THE SUMMONING

Alex,

May long drives never separate us. Lets remember where we came from, but continue to enjoy the adventure and love to come.

Sam

THE SUMMONING

S. V. FILICE

Life Rattle Press

LIFE RATTLE PRESS, 2017
Toronto, Canada

Copyright © 2017

All rights reserved. The use of any part of this publication reproduced, transmitted in any form or by any means, electronic, mechanical, photocopying, recording or otherwise, or stored in a retrieval system, without prior consent of the author is an infringement on the copyright law.

Editors
Danielle Webster
Nichelle Roberts

Book design by Samantha Filice

The Summoning / Filice, S.V
ISBN: 978-1-987936-34-6

For those who have an affinity for reading,

Chapter 1

Brett hasn't asked for much in the past couple of months. That's not to say she doesn't take things, like my favourite yellow sweater, which she's wearing now. She's been good. She listens. She just wiped her nose on the sleeve. I shake my head and keep walking, avoiding the cracks in the asphalt. In some ways, it's like nothing has changed. Except for Jeremy, who keeps peeking glances at me, half expecting me to break down on the cold sidewalk and demand his loving attention and yell how life isn't fair. We both know I'm thinking it.

"Can we go?" Brett's freckled hand thrusts a yellow water-stained flyer in my face. She pulled it from the side of a mailbox while Jeremy teased me about a grey hair.

The sun sinks behind rusted rooftops and streaks the blue sky with white trails of light. Trees shed small pink flowers and the wind blows them across the pavement. A girl, around my age, sits on a wooden bus bench close to the curb. Her blue skirt hitches up her thigh and exposes goosebumps along her skin. I look into her blotchy red eyes. She twitches and turns away.

Soon the streetlights will turn on and we'll return home late for curfew. I push myself forward. My thighs rub together and the heels of my flip-flops slap against the sidewalk. Brett skips to my side and loops her arm in mine.

"Please?"

"I said no." I rip the page from her dirty finger nails and shove it against Jeremy's chest. He shuffles to catch it.

"But what if we hear from Mom? Don't you want to hear from her?" Her eyebrows pinch together and her expression accuses me of being a crappy sister.

"Look, Brett, I miss her just as much as you do. But do you really believe this fraud can tell us something about Mom that we don't already know?"

We stop in front of Aunt Josephine's house. The white shutters and black picket fence would stand out in any romance novel, but not in the suburban neighbourhood of Feathercoe. Every house has identical flowerbeds planted under the windowsills, matching green lawns and red painted garage doors. There are no mounted basketball hoops on the neighbouring tiled brick driveways and no abandoned bikes on sidewalks. It doesn't matter how long I've lived at Aunt Jo's, I always walk past it. To help, Brett suggests I count four from the corner to make it easier, but I never care to put in the effort.

Aunt Jo's pointy nose peeks between the white lace curtains of the kitchen window. Her brown hair is wound in a tight bun, tugging her skin and erasing her laugh lines. Her face is the same plump shape as my father's and mine. Aunt Jo never had kids of her own, so Brett and I are something she can't relate to. Always hovering around the corner and listening by the doorframe is how Aunt Jo fulfills her role as our guardian—making sure we're not trouble, but hiding in case we are. I face my back towards her, attempting to use my body as a shield from her ears.

"I don't know, Isabelle, it sounds pretty cool." Jeremy adds. I round on him, but his palms are already up. He points to where Aunt Jo waits as if he is trying to warn me that I should watch my tone. I'm unsure if he's more concerned for me or if the image of being chased by a lady in hair rollers and a wooden spoon still haunts him. I decide I don't care.

"You're supposed to be on my side!" My hands fling in the air before they rest on my hips. He reads the flyer to me as if I didn't hear Brett recite the same words all afternoon.

Crystal: Spiritualist & Palm Reader.

"You really believe in this stuff?" I reach for the stained paper and try to make out the messy scrawl that says the street name.

"Hey, if Brett wants to go, I'll take her, but if cool voodoo shit happens and you miss it, I don't want to hear a word." Jeremy puffs out his chest and flashes the movie-star grin he learned from two summers in acting class, but we don't talk about his Travolta phase.

"Voodoo shit? That's our mother! And besides, wherever my sister goes, I go." I turn towards the house and Aunt Jo shifts away from the curtain to appear less obvious. I roll my eyes.

"So we're going! Oh my gosh, thanks, Jer!" Brett runs up the cracked concrete steps and into the house, slamming the white splintered door in front of me. I clutch the flyer tighter.

I face Jeremy on the wooden porch. He's already sitting on the black wired love seat. I know he's trying to make my sister happy, but taking care of her has become a habit of ours the past four months.

"I don't think it's healthy for her to rely on some stranger's made-up encounter with our mother. I want Brett to feel grateful for the memories she already has instead of communicating with someone who's not her." I curl up next to him and pull my knees to my chin. His arm falls around my waist and his fingers trail against the ruffled fabric of my shirt.

"I think it will help her. She wants to know that your mom's doing okay, wherever she is." He murmurs into my thick curls. "And hey, if it's complete horse shit, we leave. It's that simple." I don't feel his lips against my hair, but I hear the sound of his kiss.

I focus on my chipped blue toenails and scuffed flip-flops. My lip juts out in a pout and I try to catch it with my teeth, "You do so much for us."

"That's why I'm here, angel. You need a male figure around." He laughs into my shoulder, but his teasing hangs between us in silence. The image of my father still sits fresh on my mind. Dad stands grave-faced next to my mother's closed casket. He left the next morning.

Jeremy nudges me. I don't respond.

The pink sky changes the white walls to orange.

I rub my wrists against my hard lashes and stifle a yawn. Brett sleeps in a heap of blankets across from me in her twin bed. I tiptoe around the brown boxes of her junk as I make my way to the washroom. Maybe orange walls would make this place a little more vibrant.

"Why are you up?" Brett croaks behind me. I pause in the doorway and stare at her haystack hair. Mom's hair did the same thing in the morning.

"Stay in bed. I need to search train times and call Jer." Her blue eyes brighten and I know she's about to fight off sleep to come join me. I wave her off. "I'll come wake you up when it is time to leave." She smiles one of those dimpled grins that allows me to believe she can be happy again. I clutch the door frame harder and lean in. Brett collapses onto the mattress and pulls the covers over her head. Some things really don't change.

Chapter 2

"This isn't right." I say, deciphering the smudged address aloud and examining what looks like an abandoned house.

253 Devange Street.

The discoloured green wooden house stands sad at the edge of a brown lawn. Greying shingles slant and sway with each gust of wind. Cracked windows show no evidence of light from inside. I shove the flyer into the back pocket of my jeans. "Wait here," I warn Brett. My feet trip over the weeded walkway as I shuffle towards the screen door and knock through the ripped mesh netting.

I tap my foot, looking over my shoulder to wink at Jeremy. He slings an arm around Brett's neck; she crosses hers over her chest. I bite my lip and knock again. I spent our allowance of twenty dollars to get us here with Jeremy promising to pay for the ride home. I pull the crumpled flyer from my pocket and unfold it, reading for any listed dates that could hint that we're late. I glance up as the train travels into the distance between the leaves of tall maple trees and try to remember if it runs hourly.

The sun beats down and my neck perspires under the weight of my thick hair. My stomach twists at the thought of waiting in a forest for the next ride. The isolated train station is roofless, offering no shade from the sun or protection from the birds that circle overhead. The wooden platform is coin operated, abandoned by its builders and left for whoever dares to travel this far from Feathercoe. Neighbouring houses are tucked under moss blankets, forgotten by civilization, but convenient for the lifestyle of a psychic.

I turn and slide away from the door. It creaks open behind me. I twitch, startled as I whirl to face the shadow behind the torn screen. Frail grey fingers clutch the trim of the frame as if she relies on it for support. She smiles yellow teeth and squints from under her thick curved lenses and blue eyeshadow. Her wrinkled face droops and displays a maze of her years.

"Crystal?" I ask, mentally punching myself for imagining someone younger.

Brett runs up the steps, clutching Jeremy's long sleeve and shoves me to the side. I grab her wrist, tugging her away from the stranger before she gets too close. Brett glares at me under her short blonde-streaked hair. It sticks flat just shy of her shoulders as if to mock me for not waking her up earlier this morning to shower.

"I'm Brett." She turns to beam at the lady. "Tell her you're Crystal." She nods towards me like I don't have a name.

"That's no way to introduce someone, darling, especially not to your sister. However, I am Crystal." She holds her hand out to me. I grip it. The loose skin slides under my fingertips and her long metallic nails dig into my knuckles.

"How did you know?" I point at Brett. She has Mom's light features where mine mirror Dad's. Our similarities stop at our narrowed jaws and round eyes. I would swap my plump cheeks and half my weight in thighs for her slender legs and high cheekbones.

Crystal nods, ignoring my question as she gestures us inside. "Come in." I glance at Jeremy who shrugs and shuffles around Crystal. His tall frame towers over her frail body. I reach for Brett's wrist again before she can step over the threshold. Crystal raises her thin eyebrows.

"I'm sorry," I reply, unsure why I should apologize for offending a stranger after she invites us into her creepy house.

"Would you like my services in communicating with your mother?" She drops her chin and peers at me from over her lenses.

"Okay, now, how did you know that?" I ask. Brett shakes my arm in excitement.

"It's my job to know, darling." She sighs. Crystal walks away from the door, not waiting for us to follow. I let go of Brett's wrist and shield my arm in front of her, willing myself to go first so she can have time to get away just in case. I pull out my phone to check the service and nod—four bars.

The unpolished wooden floors turn dull under my feet as I step deeper into the old house. The tarnished trail marks the pathway of previous visitors. Cream-coloured sheets cover old furniture to prevent dust from settling. Jeremy leans against the staircase. He swaps his weight between his feet until we approach. His arm grips around my waist and he watches me study the room.

A faint yellow light gleams from a doorway at the end of the hall. A red beaded curtain drapes the frame and shines a pattern of jewels against the floor. Crystal ushers inside and we stumble through. The beaded wire strands shake and crackle together.

The room is a mix of gold and red. A circular table is set up with a candle centerpiece and ruby runner. Engraved symbols mark the glossy wood surface in a lined pattern. A wool rug covers the floor, spun together with alternating shades of metallic yellows. Bordering the blood-red wall is an apothecary table filled with glass fixtures. The jars are stuffed with odd shapes, some appear herbal and others cloudy from the moisture of wet objects. Ew.

A chair screeches against the floor. It shoots across the room and cuts off the exit. I jump and reach for Brett. A small shadow nudges the leg of the table and races through the doorway. The candle wobbles and blows out.

"A cat," Jeremy whispers in my ear.

"Yes, that would be Aiyana," Crystal stares after her cat the way a mother would silently scold her misbehaving child in front of guests. She clicks her tongue and reaches for a match to relight the centerpiece. "Shall we proceed? Please, take a seat." She opens her palm towards the large table.

"Hate to state the obvious, but there's only three chairs." Jeremy balls his fists in his pockets and toes the wood with his feet the way he always does when he feels he has to let someone down.

"I much prefer to stand," Crystal gestures to the seats again and this time everyone follows. "Now, you dear, how old are you?" She hovers behind Brett and reaches down for her wrist, prying open her fingers. Crystal thumbs the lines on Brett's flat palm and her long silver nails work to read the meaning.

"I'm twelve," Brett replies. She sticks her chin up to defend any chance of Crystal calling her a child.

"Much too young to lose your mother," Crystal nods.

"And my dad," Brett clenches her jaw and stares between where Jeremy and I sit. She refuses to make eye contact. I open my mouth, but Crystal waves me into a silence. I snap my lips shut and squirm in my seat. My fingers itch to reach across the table.

"Yes, yes, so your mother mentions how strong you both have been. What great responsibility your sister has taken." I shoot a scowl at Jeremy that says, *Is she for real?* He shrugs in agreement. I know he's waiting for voodoo shit to start. "Your sister, Isabelle isn't it?" Crystal glances over to me as she continues to thumb Brett's palm. My eyelids droop and my lips purse. "She has a hard time believing in what I do, doesn't she?" I fiddle with my thumbs on the table, no longer able to bring myself to meet her stare. "Maybe we should start with an exercise."

"Yeah, show her how your powers work!" Brett chimes. She scoots her seat backwards and wiggles until she's comfortable. Determined to have the best spot for the show.

"Not powers, they're affinities. I'm able to draw on spirit and the energy in your blood." Brett's eyebrows pull together as she tries to find the relation to Crystal's job description. She shrugs, finding whatever the fraud says justifiable. "What do you say, then?" Crystal exposes her yellow teeth to me.

I flatten my palms against the table and raise a single brow. "Let's do it."

A makeshift lantern sits in the middle of the table. It burns foreign herbs in thick clouds that clump above our heads. I resist the urge to cough to demonstrate obvious concern for Crystal's fire and safety precautions, but I remain quiet, staring at the light of the lantern like she instructs. Maybe she should open a window.

"Now, this is an exercise to test your Sight, which I hope will open you up to your affinities someday." Crystal circles around the table. She stops behind my chair as if to direct her next words to me. "Some struggle with the simple Sight of Knowing. They cannot distinguish right from wrong easily because they rely on greater facts that are sometimes too broad." At the centre of the table, the flame wisps and slithers. I blink to focus and it's gone. Crystal maneuvers her way behind Jeremy. The top of her grey braid sweeps short of the smoke that lingers above us. "Others struggle with the Voice of Reason. They cannot lead because they do not believe they hold such strength." My eyes widen as the flame takes the shape of running hooves. I attempt to break my gaze and glance over the lantern to see if Brett notices, but my vision is stuck on the fog picture. I can't look away as the flame morphs into the outline of a train. "And finally, others struggle with the Touch of Force. They do not know when to apply effort singularly because they split it amongst many things."

Crystal rests her silver nails on Brett's chair. "Ah, dear, you did have a short lifeline." Crystal lowers her voice, muttering a form of prayer I cannot decipher. "Let the exercise begin."

Brett falls slack in her chair. I watch with wide eyes as her neck lolls uncomfortably. Jeremy's head thuds against the table and I'm unable to move. Pressure squeezes my temples before I can find an escape.

"No!" but it's barely a whisper.

Chapter 3

A rattle sounds in the distance and a hiss rings in my ear. A twig snaps beside my head. I open my eyes and find myself lying in the dirt between long, thin-bladed grass and a moss covered boulder. Trees guard the sun and the wind guides the leaves, casting square patterns of light around me.

I sit up, my palms digging into the wet earth. Small, sharp stones imprint the tough skin of my elbows. I shove myself onto my knees and the memory of a rising flame fills my mind as it slithers into the vision of nature around me. A short hiss echoes and I jump to my feet. My flip-flops are missing and my jeans are ripped and smudged with dirt.

"Brett?" I whisper. "Brett!" My voice breaks the silence. The wind loosens a few leaves and they fall around me, gliding gently in a way that would have made me gawk if I knew the promise of safety still applied.

The train left Jeremy, Brett and me only a short walk from Crystal's. Unlike Aunt Jo, Crystal lived in seclusion surrounded by trees and the soft hum of nature. All would have been alluring if she did not live so close to a train track. The woods that engulfed her house went on for miles. My short legs suddenly feel insignificant next to the aged trees above me. Jeremy. My pulse flutters. Did he find Brett and take her to safety?

The hiss sounds again and this time it's longer. My heart pounds and my palms turn clammy. I trudge away, shuffling through the waist-high grass and uneven dirt ground. I take a breath and listen for the train, hoping to hear the distant sound of civilization. I strain to catch the rattle of wheels on rusting tracks and screeching brakes, but all that comes is the crack of twigs and the creak of hollowing branches. I trek farther, aiming for the slight elevation ahead and hope for the advantage of height. I have to remain calm. I have to find Brett.

"Hello!" I yell. Silence answers.

I don't know how long I can walk. My limbs are sore and the hissing grows irritated. Louder and longer as if beckoning me to notice. It doesn't stop. Neither do I. I glance over my shoulder, walk backwards a few strides, then turn around and continue straight. I speed up, my toes digging into the wet earth. The high ground exposes nothing but more trees. My thick hair hangs in knots down my spine and sweat forms between my shoulder blades. My eyes droop and my throat feels dry.

"Use the Sight of Knowing. Find the Deception and get rid of it and you will find freedom." Crystal's voice touches me with the light breeze as if the air carried her words to me.

I glance around, circling in search for Crystal. A shadow dodges between two large wooden trunks and I lunge for it. The whim of adrenaline pushes me farther. The soles of my bare feet tear against exposed stems and small rocks. The pain numbs itself against the hope of freedom. I enter between the trees where the shadow hid. I stand alone.

"I found the Deception and it's gone." I cry out and crumple to my knees in the shade. My cheek presses against the cold dirt. I lie there and close my eyes. I pray Brett is safe and Crystal punishes only me for being a nonbeliever. My tears moisten the ground.

Time passes, but there's no way of telling how long.

A hiss sounds in my ear and something slides over my hair. My chest shudders and I leap to my feet. A black stubbed tail retracts into the shrubs around the trunk of a tree. If I wasn't scared or alone in a forest, I'd laugh at the irony of a snake as the concept of deception. Now I know. My knees tremble as I reach for a small branch. I have to get rid of it.

I poke at the fallen leaves, moving them to expose the disgusting scales of the Deception's face. Its skin gleams in the light as its thick body swivels and slides over the dirt. I grip the branch like a club, readying myself. It slithers forward and snaps. I jump, losing my footing and swinging my arms to catch my fall. I drop the stick in exchange for balance. Its yellow eyes stare at me as it rises and sways the way the flame flared before it vanished. "Find the Deception and get rid of it," I whisper to myself.

I crouch, keeping my gaze levelled with the snake's as I lower myself. I coax it with one hand as I reach with the other for the fallen stick. The snake watches my palm with a tilted head as my fingers scramble against the dirt, catching flakes under my nails. I feel the tough bark of the branch and pull it towards me with a jerk that causes the snake to lunge. But I'm quicker. The snake exposes its sharp teeth, expanding its throat as it dives towards my neck. The adrenaline rushes through me as I shift my weight and arch forward. My body steers sideways with confident speed and my feet plant in the dirt for balance. I lodge the stick inside its mouth and push with all my strength. The branch protrudes as a swollen lump behind the snake's throat before it breaks free through the scales. The snake gives a final hiss and falls to the ground.

I scurry backwards through the debris with my palms and feet until I feel fresh bark press against my back. I heave ragged breaths, gulping at the air to slow my breathing. The black carcass of the snake seems small in the wide clearing. It twitches and I gasp. My freedom didn't come because it's not dead. A cold shiver shakes my body in the summer's heat. I pat my damp cheeks and swat at the leftover tears. My eyes always water when I'm scared. I rest my elbows on my knees and wipe the hair that sticks to my neck with my muddy hands.

The snake convulses and rises, but this time it's different. Its black scales are faded, almost transparent as it swerves and dances. Its mouth moves to hiss, but no sound escapes. A thick layer of dark fog clumps together to form the swift movements of the snake one last time and then releases into a thin distorted cloud.

The breeze carries the Deception away. It floats high into the atmosphere, between the trees and above the clearing. The fog reflects the image of a slithering snake and the wind blurs it until it disappears. I sit for a while, gaping at the empty body still at my feet.

My head falls into my clammy palms and everything goes dark.

Chapter 4

I wake up with a sweaty cheek stuck to a laminated wood table. Magnified grey eyes smile at me through thick lenses. Crystal.

"Dear, you did it." Her wrinkled touch nudges me from my exhaustion. I flinch, scooting away from the table to put some distance between us. My foot snags on the chair leg when I try to stand. I stumble forward. My body tingles. My feet are numb from sleep. I examine the room, the other two chairs are empty. I glance down at my clothes. My flip-flops are on my feet and my jeans are clean. Any evidence of mud and the forest were washed away with sleep.

I reach into my pocket and grab my rubber phone case. It sticks to the fabric of my pants. No new messages. I remember the absence of its weight against my leg in the forest. I could have called for help if I had it. I study the screen more closely to catch the numbers that fade into a picture of Brett smiling on the train with me and Jeremy leaning together in the background.

4:23 PM. Damn, Aunt Jo is going to kill me.

"Where's my sister?" I round on her. My voice comes out harsh. I don't apologize.

"They already left." Crystal places her lips together in a thin line and studies me. "Aren't you going to ask about the exercise? Your friend Jeremy had a lot to say." She lowers her chin towards me.

"Jeremy is not a friend." I snap.

"Very well. But I must say you handled the exercise with great knowledge. Some take longer. The Sight is a hard thing to discover for those who don't have it." With a metallic nail, she slides her lenses down the bridge of her nose for a better look, but I'm already aiming for the beaded wires.

"Listen, it was fun. I believe in your powers now and whatever voodoo shit Jeremy saw I hope he didn't leave disappointed. Now, if you'll excuse me I have to find my sister." I hear the clunk of Crystal's slippers as she trails behind me.

"Dear, do you not understand? Your journey to finding your Sight begins. You need more exercises and hopefully you'll gain your affinity." Her voice sounds grave as if not gaining my affinity is a major devastation.

I reach the door and whirl around, throw a wad of fives at her red slippers, and roll my eyes. "In case Jeremy didn't pay you." I smirk and grab the rusty knob. The peeling paint pricks at my fingers. "When's the next train?"

She nods. "Seven minutes, it will pull up on the West end."

I yank the screen door open and the mesh dangles limply. Dandelions stick out from the concrete walkway. The door slams and the house returns to its abandoned stupor. I pull out my phone and send a text to Jeremy.

```
On my way. I hope you enjoyed your
voodoo shit because I assure you it
will never happen again. xo
```

Chapter 5

I cross my arms and play with the holes on the cuffs of my sleeves. The wind picks up and blows loose curls around my face. I claw at the thick black curtain of hair and try to tame it in my cardigan hood. It's four thirty and the train hasn't come.

I feel antsy as I watch the minutes pass without receiving a text from Jeremy. The knot in my stomach thrashes and tightens at the thought of them experiencing something similar to what I encountered. I try not to feel angry at Jeremy for leaving me. Maybe he wanted to get Brett to safety, but still, he left me with a lunatic.

I pace the top of the wooden deck made for passengers to enter and exit the train's doors with ease. I wonder why such accommodations were made in a place where no crowd is expected. I settle on the lone bench in the vacant terminal, staring at the layer of filth on my feet. The dirt path to the train platform left dust clouds with each step. I kick off my flip-flops. The straps leave light traces where the dirt could not reach. A train horn sounds and I stand, stuffing my feet against the rubber soles of my flip-flops.

It approaches the West wing and, without thinking, I take Crystal's directions. I tread up the platform, scrunching my toes to grip my flip-flops. The train car is almost empty aside from a few stragglers. I didn't expect people to travel this far out of the city, but it still makes me uneasy to board without Brett or Jeremy to keep me company. I don't look up from the dirt-caked mat as I make my way to the closest seat. The ceramic chair molds uncomfortably into my back. A pair of red sneakers tap against the floor in front of me and an electric-blue stiletto nudges up and down his black jeans. I don't sit alone.

I glance up to see they're already staring at me. I nod and avert my gaze. She whispers in his ear behind a veil of her red hair and he shrugs, keeping his green eyes on my face. "You don't know where you're going, do you?" His voice came out like a huff, each word morphing into the next and causing me to stare at him for a moment. I peek at the girl with red hair beside him. She waits for my reply as well. Her eyes are dark, almost black against her vibrant hair.

He leans forward, curious to hear what I have to say. "I'm going home to Feathercoe." I don't see why it's his business what town I live in.

"Good luck," And he means it. He rests his head against the wall and blinks. His foot taps to an unheard rhythm. The red-haired girl nuzzles under his chin and stares quietly out the window.

I glance down at my phone and find no reply from Jeremy. He's probably too busy calming the wrath of Aunt Jo to message me. A part of me, the larger, more hopeful one, says he's keeping Brett entertained until I get there.

I watch the trees thin and the track twist into a single rail. The solid dirt ground turns to low brick fencing and the green forest morphs to blue water. The train glides effortlessly and I gape at the window across from me. The rails are no longer visible from where I sit, making it appear as if the train is floating across the blue expanse.

"Wait. This is the wrong way! Where are we going?" I yell at the guy across from me, the one with red shoes. The girl with blue stilettos smiles, but pays me no regard. The guy narrows his eyes and nods, taking me into consideration.

"Bible camp," the girl with red hair snickers. The guy rolls his eyes.

"Bible camp?" I repeat.

"I knew you were one of them when you hopped on the train." He wags a finger at me.

"One of what? What the hell are you talking about? Where are we going? Town is the other way!" I stand, pushing at his finger to make him take it back.

"How comfortably you can speak of Hell." The girl watches me with amusement.

"Not now, Onyx." The boy lifts a palm towards her. He looks at me and nods again. "How I wish I was so fortunate to be like the blind, having it easy and receiving closer care."

"I'm not blind. I can see you." I shake my head and plop down into my seat.

"Ah, but you don't know what I am." He slouches against the chestnut-coloured bench and crosses his arms.

"What do you mean? Like gay?" I frown at the girl, Onyx, slumped under his armpit. I guess it could be friendly.

"Gay?" He scoffs. "Do I look gay?" he asks Onyx and she shrugs.

"Okay, I don't care if you are. I just want to get home." I cross my arms and sit up straighter, challenging him.

"Darling, you're not going home." His voice is cool. He lifts his hands as if to say nothing can change this unfortunate circumstance and he doesn't give a damn that I'm part of it.

"I'm not going home? Can't I just hop off and change trains to take one going in the other direction?" I glance out the window at the one-way track. "What about my sister, then? She was at Crystal's with me! And Jeremy? Oh God, he'll flip!" Unable to get comfortable, I stand up again and settle for pacing the car.

"So you weren't alone?" Onyx asks. "Ash, do you know what this means?" She turns to the boy and I watch them for a moment. Onyx and Ash. Really?

"Hopefully that witch didn't send them on the wrong train, too." I pace back and forth with heavy feet, twirling a strand of hair between my fingers. "I have to get home, Aunt Jo won't know when to feed Brett, even her plants are dying!" I drop my hands with a thud. Oh God, would Jeremy order pizza?

"Crystal isn't a witch. She's an Exorcist." Onyx snickers.

"Exorcist? Like she takes demons out of people? But we're not possessed." I stop pacing and rub my temples. I dismiss the idea with a long blink. This girl has definitely spent too many late nights reading fan-fiction.

"How little you know. It's cute." Onyx smirks. "Exorcists don't remove demons from your body—that can't be done. Everyone is born with some lightness and some darkness, you know that little good angel–bad angel deal you grew up believing? Yeah, well, an Exorcist is situated to find those cases where the good is still saveable. And when it's not, well, that's where your Hollywood theories come in. The demon consumes you and takes over the little humanity you have and that's that. If your body can't fight it... Think of it this way, have you ever heard of anyone surviving an exorcism?" I try to remember all the Halloweens I spent up late watching scary movies with Jeremy. I shake my head.

"So then what's the point of Crystal's job if they can't be saved?" I stare into Onyx's black eyes, hoping the answers are written there. I sit down in front of her and lean forward, pleading her for help. If what Onyx says is true, I need to stop this. I have to find Brett.

"Crystal's duty isn't to save them, but to tally them on the map. She can sense when a soul is too weak, the amount of angel lineage left in your blood or if it has worn away over generations. Those who have less of a tie to their ancestors are easier to take." Onyx shrugs away from Ash who stares at me from across the car.

"Angel lineage? I don't even go to church." I scoff. "Angels can't possibly exist." I think of Mom and how her fair-hair rippled like a halo in the sun. If Heaven exists, I know she's there. But this can't be real. Black curls sweep above my waistline as I twirl to examine the other empty seats. Who are these people?

"Well, start praying, Sweetheart." Ash says. Onyx silences him with a nudge, motioning for him to give me time to digest her stories. A prank, that's what this is. Two people taking advantage of finding a girl on the wrong train and getting a good laugh.

But something in their eyes lacks humour. I know they believe what they tell me.

My skin starts to prickle.

"So that's what Crystal meant when she said she has an affinity with bloodlines? She knows if we have good blood or if the bad blood is stronger? She was checking to see if me and my sister were demons!" I almost shout. My mind whirls and I hunch forward, dabbing my forehead to test for a fever.

"Well, there's not really bad blood, it is neutral. The darkness in us is from being blind or unknowing and giving into temptation. That kind of stuff." Onyx nods in approval, impressed I'm not freaking out. Well, that she can see.

"Crystal told me I lack in the Sight of Knowledge. Does that mean I'm more likely to change into a demon?" I watch her expression for any sorrow or pity, but it remains unreadable.

"Sight of Knowing," she corrects. "Did she perform the ritual?"

As much as I want to ask what Onyx meant by the ritual, I know it was the whole voodoo shit I experienced. I sum up my encounter with the snake and she listens, patiently decoding my experience, but not daring to share more information. She leans into Ash and nestles closer.

"Good, then you're not a demon." Her mocking tone carries little humour.

"Listen, sweetheart, you better hope your sister and friend are on a train somewhere because if the Exorcist didn't see their strength, they won't make it to month's end. That ritual provides Sight to darkness as well as light. It's the reason you're able to understand what Onyx is telling you, your blood knows the truth. And if the darkness finds knowledge, it feeds. There's a reason why light is symbolized as a flame. It takes work to remain lit and when it goes out, darkness is waiting to consume." Ash speaks in a clear voice. It echoes off the train's walls, carrying weight with each word.

I nod.

One line repeats over in my mind, *You better hope your sister and friend are on a train somewhere because if the Exorcist didn't see their strength, they won't make it to month's end.*

Chapter 6

I sit in silence for the rest of the ride, asking few questions about angel blood and ancestors. Apparently, no one knows where their bloodline originates. Where you descend from starts in the section of the Bible when the angels first fell. The Fallen mated with humans the first couple hundred years and left the bearing mothers to beg for forgiveness in Heaven, abandoning their children for duty. The women then conceived and the goodness in blood thinned through generations. That's why exorcisms are more common now. Exorcists try to save those with weak ties to light because the more worn the bloodline the more vulnerable someone is to darkness. This is how Onyx summarized it for me.

I ask her how she knows all this stuff and when she received her Sight and more importantly, if there was a snake in her dream. She tells me everyone's exercise is different depending on how your mind perceives. She mentions how she and Ash were born with Sight.

"How are you born with it? I thought it's something you acquire over the years like affinities?" I sit beside Onyx and cross my legs on the hard bench.

"Some people need to work towards Sight, others need to strengthen it. There are four categories. The Sight of Knowing, Voice of Reason, Touch of Force and Sound of Truth. All are kind of self-explanatory." She watches me bite my lip. Her black-leather clad shoulders shrug. "You'll catch on once we get to camp."

"Camp? So we're actually going to Bible camp?" I ask and peer out the window. Onyx snorts and Ash shakes his head.

The water stretches on as the train steers forward. I sneak a glance at Ash who taps his foot aimlessly. Onyx doesn't clarify where we are going and I'm sure it's because Ash restricts the amount of details she's allowed to spill. *Tempore* is what he mutters when Onyx gets ahead of herself. *In time.*

"I keep forgetting you weren't brought up on a reserve!" Onyx says. A reserve is a secluded place where those who have higher concentrations of angel blood are raised. Their family ties are stronger because they grew up with the truth, whereas in heavier packed populations the knowledge of our ancestors fade. This is why I lack Sight. Some are not strong enough to understand their Knowledge and Exorcists like Crystal watch over those numbers. Onyx continues, "If you lack balance in your Senses, whether they are all at a low level or high, you are sent to a camp to train. Crystal saw you lacked Sight, but understood you are strong enough to learn more. This train leads to Knowledge and there you will work on all Senses to remain balanced, but also strengthen your Sight." Ash quits tapping his red sneakers and aimlessly loops a strand of Onyx's hair around his thumb. His green eyes watch the trail it leaves between his fingertips.

"What about affinities? Do we learn those at school, too?" I continue to watch Ash, his black hair cropped too short for him to play with.

"It's not a school," Onyx scolds. "No, affinities are different. They surface on their own time. It's something your blood excels in, a little gift from your ancestors. Everyone's works differently because we all have different genes, but many are similar or categorized. Most get their affinity at the end of training, other's get them sooner and go straight into a field of work." She stops my protests, "Each job is different, all jobs help balance. Some recruit, some regulate and others are more hands-on." Onyx winks. I have a feeling those who are hands-on aren't fixing plumbing.

"Do you have an affinity?" I ask. Ash drops Onyx's hair and then recovers his rhythm almost as if his fumble took part of the beat.

"No, I don't," Onyx mumbles but her eyes deepen to the same black as her pupils. "You better make sure you have everything, we're almost there." She nods towards the duffle bags I never noticed above us on the barred racks. I glance around. I have nothing to carry. The phone in my pocket feels hot against my leg. The image of my sister smiling on the train flashes in my mind and I dismiss it.

Tempore.

Chapter 7

I don't know what I expected when the train stopped. Maybe small dragons running around or even someone to greet us and clarify our mission in life, but nope, there's none of that. Patted-down sand and brown columned buildings stand in front of the platform.

The sandy ground stretches into a vacant lot. In the corner, an isolated patch of grass grows beneath wooden park benches. The square is mowed down to dry dead grass and pebbles. The hard ground extends to the tree line behind the buildings. Bordering the area sits three housing structures. The sun glints off of the smooth marble roofing. I trail behind Onyx and Ash who sound off their names as if they studied the layout before.

"—the Meeting Square… ah yes, Ordnance, Doctrine and Residence. I expected it to be much bigger."

"Ash, you know this is one of the smaller camps. Maybe we should have gone overseas like your father said. I'm sorry you had to come here." Onyx latches on to Ash's arm and rests against his swollen bicep.

"It's my choice." He leads her forward and I follow.

"Where is everyone?" I flinch at the way my voice carries over the vacant field. Ash called it the Meeting Square yet no one seems to meet here. And it's a rectangle.

"According to what we were taught, the four Preceptors know when new Descendants arrive. They are to meet us here, in the Meeting Square." Onyx peers at me and rolls her eyes. "Four Preceptors, one for each of the Senses. They monitor the balance of each Descendent." *Duh.* She doesn't say it, but the sentence feels more complete this way.

"The other Descendants should be in either Ordnance or Doctrine depending on their schedule. They will be off for dinner soon," Ash adds, his face is uninterested in reciting facts as his eyes sweep every building, studying the grandness of their shape and architecture. "This place has been around for a very long time."

"Since 1584 when America started to populate. Before, camps were remote and this was one of the first established. Less people meant less of a balance to maintain. To arrive, it took days to travel rather than the few hours you experienced. Also, people were more balanced then." The voice comes from beside me and I whirl to stare. He walks in front of two men, one with a glossy bald head and the other seems to have confiscated his share of hair as it whips out behind him in a ponytail. "I am Caradoc." He wears a long chestnut duster that capes around his ankles and brings out the flecks of brown in his silver hair. "This is Peter and Julius." Caradoc gestures to the bald man, then to the one with the ponytail. His voice has a hint of a British accent around the "er" of "Peter." He sings the vowels of each word. "Zilla is finishing up in Doctrine and will arrive shortly. Do forgive her." He gestures at the large building in front of us. So that is Doctrine, huh?

A doorway is hollowed out from the centre of the stone wall and morphs into a hall that tunnels the length of the building. Shadows conceal how deep the walls run. Dark rectangles mark the sides of the hallway suggesting either adjacent rooms or more exits. None of them have doors. The building towers higher than the rest and has windows only on the top floor. They appear as tiny squares cut into the brown stone of the walls. Doctrine curves into a half-moon shape with two protruding corridors that flank the perimeter of the Meeting Square. The building appears as if it were built around the empty field and stands to outline its importance.

I examine the next building, its large L shape outlines the Meeting Square the way you misplace a tile in "Tetris." The building across the field, in front of the train tracks, fills in the final gap of the square. Its rectangle structure is the least interesting, but helps to signify the length of the Square's expanse. It also appears as the most recently renovated with glass windows that span along its sides in patterned distances.

"Surely Peter and Julius can speak for themselves Caradoc." A woman in a long black cloak approaches from across the square. "My name is Zilla—I'll be leading your orientation this evening." She clasps her hands in a way that concludes things are done the way she says, which is both terrifying and promising.

The men exit the way they came and Zilla waits, studying them until they're gone. "You will come to find that inequality is laid by those who were raised in olden traditions, but we're here to shake that." She smiles and her teeth are like pearls against her dark skin. Her high cheekbones and tight features make her appear somewhat feral.

"Is that your nice way of saying Caradoc is old?" Onyx asks. She smirks her sarcastic grin and crosses her arms.

Zilla smiles with her lips. Her skin curves softly without any hint of age lines or dimples. "That, and a woman should not receive orders from a man unless he is her father." She studies Onyx's claim on Ash's arm. "But I can see you have no problem with that." She nods towards Onyx's hold as if understanding the influence the young Descendant has over her boyfriend. "Ash, I've heard much about you and I'm sure you'll find this place accommodating. Once I conclude our agenda remind me to introduce you to Aliza, she is our Excel in Sound." She bows in greeting and Ash returns it, though a little stiff. Zilla peers at me next. "Isabelle, this orientation is mainly for you. If you have any confusion, fear not to consult me. I am the Excel of Touch as well as one of the Preceptors." She walks towards the L shaped building and I catch Onyx staring after her with lifted eyebrows. She shrugs and dismisses Zilla's direct greeting towards me as only a way to confirm my ignorance to Sight, not that she is less important. Onyx doesn't need an introduction, they've studied the camp layout at the reserve.

"What's an Excel?" I whisper to Onyx as we trail behind.

"It's someone who is balanced and has mastered their affinity in a Sense. Now shh," Onyx hushes me

"This is Ordnance. You will train your Senses here through inner and physical contact." Zilla says as we enter the narrow tunnel. There are no doors to rooms just hollowed frames. I peek into an archway, but catch only a glimpse of an empty wooden desk before we rush forward. Farther down, the building branches off into other corridors. "Your classes are held here for the first of your exercises, and unlike Doctrine, all who are admitted will start in lower levels. These will test your abilities to use Senses. Each exercise is different. You will receive your schedules tomorrow." Zilla walks forward and her heels click against the stone ground.

Little light fixtures drape the wall and to my surprise they aren't torches but tiny white bulbs. After rows of rooms, we near the end of the hall where the building twists for the remaining portion of the L. The ground droops lower and then morphs into stairs. A slight chill picks up as we march down and when I start to think the narrow stairway will suffocate me, it expands into a lavish dome.

We stand at the top level—the observation deck of the arena. People sit on the bleachers that line the walls and, down in the room's centre, a boy shoots a crossbow clean into the heart of a waxwork dummy. I watch as he reloads and shoots again. "The gym is here for training and sometimes guest speakers. Of course, you may enter during your free time." She twirls around and guides us up the stairs and I peel my eyes away from the black-haired boy as he shoots again with a thud. I think of Onyx on the train saying *others are more hands-on.*

We hike up the steep steps back to the corner of the L. Zilla guides us into the shaded hall opposite from the way we came. I squint to understand where the tunnel leads, but the light dies in the distance. Ash's skin is plucked of all colour. His pale lips are clamped shut. Onyx's red brows lower and I know she's trying to concentrate on our direction. The tunnel runs in the same direction as the stairs, but where those inclined, this path remains above ground. We travel only a few feet, but it feels like minutes with the humidity. We plunge into the light and heat of the day. Sweat beads my hairline and I check my wrist for a tie. My heart retracts when I realize I gave it to Brett. Did she tour a building similar to Ordnance?

I imagine Brett when she acts fearless. How her lips press together and her thin shoulder bones protrude as she stiffens, the tendons in her arm noticeable from her delicate fisted hands. I blink to push away the sting behind my eyes.

We tread haggard strides, stepping into the sunlight for a few steps before we plummet back into the darkness of Doctrine's adjacent tunnel. Unlike Ordnance this building doesn't appear so secretive. The sun pours through carved windows and skylights. The hall ends with stone stairwells and we change course, veering left to follow the walls of the building.

"This is where you will learn theory and history, the Doctrine building. Each floor is dedicated to a Sense. The first is Touch, located close to the square and accessible to Ordnance if need be. The second is Sight, secluded on the floor that has no access to outdoor vision, which is why there are no windows. Most exercises require you to look within. The third is Voice and you may find its set up unique as it is the noisiest level because each floor reverberates upwards. Finally, there is Sound located in the towers, separated for silence. Its openness to light and wind provides easy concentration," Zilla explains. "Again, your classes are chosen for you. The less familiar will have classes at the heart of the building and work their way outward. If it helps, there are only two rooms per corridor and five corridors. Good luck," Zilla concludes as if to dismiss us, but she continues to lead down the hall. Onyx looks at Ash before settling on me. One eyebrow lifts and I shrug. I have no idea if we're supposed to follow, either.

Ash sighs and leads the way. We speed up until we reach a comfortable distance near Zilla and fall back. She doesn't check to see if we're there. I glance down each hall as we pass. Classrooms cast small flecks of light against the ground in rectangular motions. We reach the carved arch doorway that leads into the Meeting Square and Zilla stops.

"The entrance to the Square faces the centre hall where all new Descendants are situated for classes. Isabelle you are meant to find it accommodating. Stairwells are located at the East and West Tunnels like the one you saw upon entrance. As you see we are now at the Meeting Square. This is where I leave you." She lifts her palms to direct our attention to where the sun lowers. "Ash I will ask you to follow me. You are to meet with Aliza. Don't worry, I'll have you back with your friends for dinner." She smiles her feral grin at him, her eyes dancing with humour. "Isabelle and Onyx, you will meet with Julius at Residence. He will check you into your rooms. Unfortunately, boys and girls have separate living arrangements. Curfew is at eleven and dinner at seven. That provides you with an hour to settle before you have to find yourselves here in the Meeting Square." She nods one last time and heads back towards the East Tunnel. Ash follows.

Onyx stares after him, biting her lip. "I guess we better go." It's the first time I hear her sound unsure. She turns towards the Meeting Square and struts out of Doctrine.

"Do you think we'll be roommates?" I suggest, wanting to break the silence of our walk across the large sand field.

"Camp is meant to teach you balance and sometimes you realize what makes you lack it, are the certain ties you carry. They will not place you based on familiarity."

Chapter 8

I keep thinking of Brett and Jeremy. Who their roommates are and if they believe in the purpose of their camp. I remember the vivid image of a lunging snake, its lolled scaled body and then smoke. I shudder. It felt real and with every explanation I feel something click inside me, like I heard an answer I never knew I needed. No, Brett would not give in without a fight; she would react as if she were a hostage. I entertain the idea of her taking it out on whoever got suckered into rooming with her. She would never let herself cry. I know Jeremy will attempt to find balance in order to receive freedom. I plan to do the same. The camp grounds that separate us make Jeremy's protection difficult. Of course I tell myself that they're situated at a camp because I cannot bear the latter, which is the people I care about succumbed to the darkness within them.

I pull out my phone to check the service. Where the four bars were it now flashes SOS. My breath hitches in my throat and the familiar pressure surfaces behind my eyes the way it does when I'm about to cry. I study the picture on the train. In the background, I sit on the bench talking as Jeremy watches my reaction. His dark expression is unreadable, consumed by whatever pointless rant I give. Brett's greasy hair and round blue eyes shine from the bottom corner as she angles the camera for a perfect shot.

A knock thuds against my door. I shove my phone under my pillow just as it opens.

Onyx peers in. "I asked for your room number. I didn't want to sit around and do nothing. I'm down the hall." She shrugs and jerks her thumb over her shoulder. I nod and she breezes past me.

"Come in." My voice sounds hoarse and I try to remember when I last spoke. Zilla's fierceness must have stunned me into timid silence.

Onyx glances around. Her red eyebrows hitch upward. "Does anyone else live in here? What the heck?" She scoffs. She points to the bare stone walls and white cotton sheets on the neighbouring twin sized bed. "My room is covered in old rock posters. I freshened it up with a cute red duvet." She smiles, satisfied with herself.

"You said heck." I tilt my head to the side, remembering when she scolded me for speaking of Hell.

"Yeah, but I know more of it than you." She waves a hand and walks in a circle. "Aren't you going to decorate?"

"I didn't come with anything remember? I'm recruited and they didn't exactly give me time to pack." I bite my lip. I remember the boxes lining my bedroom floor at home and wonder briefly what Aunt Jo might be going through. I stop the thoughts from forming. Not now.

"Uh. Do you think we're situated in the middle of butt-fuck nowhere?" She sees my reaction and raises her palm. "Okay, yes, we don't exactly live in whatever feather city you are from."

"Feathercoe," I interject.

"Yeah, whatever, but the point is there's a town not too far from here. I saw an outline when we were on the train. Plus, there are other recruited Descendants and then there are the ones who have lived here for their whole lives." Stuck in a secluded camp without your family for your entire life, unable to find enough balance to leave. I shiver. Onyx snaps her painted blue nails at me. "Hello, Isabelle? Yeah, what do you think they do? Make you wear the same outfit every day until you're able to leave?" She rolls her eyes and plummets on the white linen sheets next to me. "We need to make this place more lively."

"Okay, and what do you suggest we do? There aren't exactly many trains that lead out of here or malls built in the middle of forests."

"Julius said if we have questions we know where to find him. I have a feeling internet isn't essential here, but I know it's somewhere. Let's go." She gets up and her blue heels rake the stone ground. "I'm not waiting until some pigtail loser walks through the door and calls me her new best friend. Dinner is in half an hour. Let's do something useful." I pat my pillow once to make sure my phone is secure and follow after her. My flip-flops are soundless next to her stilettos.

We find Julius at the front desk. Its frame is forged from the stone wall and connects with the ground. A small work nook carved out of the building. His ponytail falls over his shoulder as he reads a stack of papers. He's on post for Residence, to watch who enters and checks in. Onyx says all the Preceptors rotate duties to maintain balance. He glances up at us. His hazel eyes shine with interest and knowledge. His pale skin dimples around his cheekbones, highlighting his laugh lines and crow's feet.

"Hey, guys, what's up?" He smiles a boyish grin, and I notice that his incisor crooks slightly inward.

"Hi, sir, we were wondering if you knew where we could find clothes and other necessities. I didn't come with anything really."

"Isabelle, please call me Julius." He rushes to stand, pushing his black leather chair lazily from his desk and rolling it out from under him.

"Okay, Julius, where are you keeping the goods?" Onyx smirks and her eyelids fall lazily like she's about to expose whatever lie he'd try to conceal. I muffle a laugh but Julius doesn't seem to make the same effort. He tips his head back and a rumble erupts through his chest. The incline of his neck making him dazzle under the dangling light above. I look to Onyx. Her face has lost all of its humour. She stares at him with wide eyes.

"There's no goods. Of course, we have supply zones. You'll find toothbrushes, soaps, and training clothes there. And yes, we can order you cute outfits as well." He nudges Onyx and she blushes. She doesn't appear smug for once.

"Each recruited Descendant is given an account. Obviously recruits' accounts are greater than those who were prepared upon arrival in their first year. It will readjust at each year's end." Julius leads us down the hall. My steps are hesitant and Onyx's slightly jittered. "Here it is." We spin around the corner and the ceiling morphs into a rounded dome. Shelves layer the walls and black marker labels plastic bins.

"It's not much, but you'll realize trends won't matter as they once did." Onyx makes a gagging sound and Julius smiles. "You have three days until the next shipment of supplies, so I suggest you check the clothes we have stocked here in the meantime." He points to the large clothes hampers at the end of the room labelled *F-S*, *F-M*, *F-L*. I nod and Onyx gawks. Her eyes widen and her jaw slacks. She blinks a few times to make sure.

"Where can we order clothes? I brought my parents' Visa." She reaches in her pocket and flashes a gold plastic card.

"You use Visas at the reserve?" I ask, wondering where she would have swiped it.

"What do you think we live in? Twig homes or something?" She sees my expression and her black eyes narrow. "I do not dress like a feral child, thank you."

I'm about to rebuttal when Julius pitches in. "Unfortunately, our computers are used only by administrators. You will have to use the catalogues. Paper is easy record for us." His smile is genuine but his eyes flash with humour. "Don't worry, if you dressed feral I would have turned you away at the doors. We can't let in wild animals, this is a sacred ground." He laughs again, and Onyx blushes.

She stiffens and holds up her chin. "Okay, we're good here. Isabelle's with me and quite frankly, I don't think she'd want fashion advice from you, anyway. What is that, a cape?" Onyx points to Julius' mocha-coloured duster and his smile grows. "I never read anything about Preceptors having a dress code."

Julius mocks a hurt expression and his hands fall against his heart. "This was a gift from Caradoc!"

"Explains why you all match. You do know we're not a part of a cult, right?" She raises a red brow and his face smooths over. "I would lose it if I were you. The only one who can pull it off and still appear badass is Zilla and it's not the coat that does it. Caradoc can keep it too because he has that whole old man thing going for him." My mouth opens with a pop. Did she just dis a Preceptor in front of another? She must have realized because she stops talking and crosses her arms, willing Julius to argue against her.

He clears his throat and rolls his shoulders, wiggling himself free from his duster. His navy long-sleeve shirt hugs the muscles of his arms and chest. His black jeans and leather shoes bring a sense of casual etiquette and contrast the paleness of his skin and dark features. I stay quiet, standing in the middle of Onyx, who crosses her arms and picks her nails, and Julius, who waits for approval he refuses to ask for. I'm half in the room and I peek down the hall to calculate the distance it would take to leave.

"Better," Onyx finally says and in the same movement she's shooing him out the door. Julius bows dramatically and she rolls her eyes. He turns on his heels and walks down the grey stone hall, leaving his trench coat in Onyx's fist.

She twirls, concealing her expression from me. She taps her foot and checks the inventory of the room. Distracted with the lure of shopping, Onyx cracks her knuckles and sashays towards the plastic bins. "Okay, where to start, where to start," she says to herself. Her heels rap against the ground. "Grab an empty box, we're filling it with as much junk as you can carry." I reach for a cardboard box and shuffle my way into the domed room.

At first she tosses small things in my box such as unopened deodorant and cased toothpaste. It only starts to get heavy after the creams and shampoos. I question if I need all the scents and various exfoliants and earn myself a scowl from Onyx.

I peer into the hamper marked *F-M*; assuming the smalls would fit my torso, but not my cleavage, I settle for a medium. My chest loosens when I notice the clothes aren't unwanted hand-me-downs, but still tagged and unworn T-shirts. I shuffle through the high-neck short sleeves and Onyx digs through the extra small V-necks. I muse until she shoves her pile towards me. I stare at the fabric in my box. The image of my sister's over-stuffed boxes in Aunt Jo's bedroom flashes behind my lids. I blink. Onyx aims for the jean hamper.

"So, how old do you think Julius is?" I ask to break the silence, but instead shatter Onyx's concentration. She drops the denim waistline she carries and watches it fall. She bends down to retrieve it quickly and shrugs.

"I don't know, mid-twenties maybe? I wouldn't say over twenty-six." She goes back to reading the tags, but I can see her eyes glaze over.

"Well, how old are you?" I realize we never learned the basic facts about each other, like our age or if we preferred chocolate or vanilla. Her thin frame towers over me and I realize she looks older.

"Twenty-two." Her eyebrows pinch together as she concentrates on something else.

"I'm twenty," I say. She folds a pair of jeans and sets them aside.

"Your point?"

"He's cute." I shrug and move to retrieve my findings to place them in my bin.

"I'm with Ash." She whirls, her eyes widen and her neck flinches like I hit her. She looks away and I fumble through the rack of catalogues beside the hampers. "Oh no, you're not having those. Take these." She grabs the magazines from me and places a lump of crumpled jeans in my pile, "We'll trade. Don't worry, give me some time with this bad boy and you'll come out with more than an old cardigan and skinny jeans." I peer down at my outfit, then at hers, scrunching my forehead in a way that would make Aunt Jo burst into wrinkle lectures.

We walk away from the supply dome and towards the front desk. Onyx focuses her stare ahead and talks meaninglessly about dinner and socializing to get our ranks up. Whatever that means. Julius' eyes follow us as we continue to our dorms. I drop Onyx off and count the numbers on the doors until I recognize mine.

I shuffle through the wooden frame, bump the knob with my hip, and fumble under the weight of the cardboard box. My new belongings rattle and clink together. It's only when I place them at my feet do I realize I'm not alone.

Chapter 9

He stands up from his bed with stiff shoulders, his muscles flex in a way that seems menacing. A strand of hair falls loose in front of his dark eyes and I'm left wondering if they're more black than brown.

"Well, at least all your stuff fits in that tiny box because now it won't be so hard to remove yourself from my room." His dark eyes spark from under his lashes and his full pink lips press together. I would have cringed at his coldness if I wasn't so mad at the fact that he had a symmetrical face when I didn't.

"I, uh…" I study the room and analyze the plain white cotton sheets and bare walls. "Your room?" Hell, I thought I lucked out and didn't have a roommate.

"Yeah, and if it weren't for the strict gender rules I may consider you as a roommate. You are a girl, right?" He smirks and I grind my teeth. "Should I take it up with Julius, tell him I'm getting kind of lonely? He would consider it as long as you don't try and seduce me in my sleep."

"I have a boyfriend," I say quickly, mirroring Onyx's response from earlier. He raises his eyebrows and his smirk tightens.

I flip a wad of curls to the other side of my head, a nervous habit I adopted when I finally outgrew my front bangs. I glance around the empty room, resting my eyes on the sack of arrows that weren't in the corner earlier. My gaze snaps up to the boy, his black eyes watch me with interest. His hair falls in a dark halo and I rake over the muscles in his arms. My brows pinch together.

"Are you checking me out?" He smirks lazily and I wonder if he ever shows his teeth.

"You're the one from the gym, the one in Ordnance." My head tilts to the side. It wasn't meant as a question and he knows it. I wait for his reply, one he doesn't feel like giving. "I saw you shoot," I continue. His arms tighten around his torso.

"Yeah, well, I've had a lot of practice." He shrugs, refusing to uncross his arms and bare his chest.

"I never said you were good." I cross my arms to copy his stance. My back straightens and I'm willing to put up a front of bravado if he is.

"Wasn't I?" He lifts an eyebrow and I realize this isn't a facade for him, he actually means it. He shot clean into the heart of the dummy and then the head, not once wavering as he lined up the next.

I bend down to pick up my box, not giving him the satisfaction of knowing my answer. "Lift with your knees, you're going to strain yourself." He rushes to stop me and touches my arm. I jump and lose my grip on the box, flinging it at his legs. He catches the weight in a swift movement. A few shirts topple out and land at his feet in a crumpled heap. He balances the box in one arm and bends to retrieve the fallen items with the other. I gawk at how effortless he does it. My arms race towards my stuff without any direction, grasping at fabric and skin, feeling embarrassed that he saw what was inside.

"I got it," I snap and turn towards the door. My arm tingles from his touch and I want to scream at myself for my clumsiness. "Let's go find Julius so I can unload my stuff in a room that's occupied by something more than a snob and linen sheets."

"What's wrong with my sheets?" He closes the door behind him and fiddles the key I didn't know we had. My nose wrinkles as the lock clicks shut.

"Really, how long have you lived here? If I were Julius I don't think I would have believed the memo that said this room is occupied, either." I shuffle under the weight of the box, my arms rotating between which got the worst of the load.

"I like my room. It's less to clean." I catch the sight of him behind me, his shoulders heave and fall. I guess an empty room would be.

"You didn't answer my question." I glance at him. The bulge of his jaw bone is softened by his narrow temple. His nose juts into a perfect point. His cheek bones protrude and make his eyes appear hollow under the casted shadows. Brown. His eyes are brown.

"You never answered mine." He raises an eyebrow and sighs, stepping around me to pass. We trail down the stone stairs in silence. He mutters to himself, but stops to glare at me.

We round the corner and find ourselves in the front hall. I glance over at the stairwell and notice Onyx and I followed a different path on our trip up the first time. My arms shake and I grip the box tighter, not wanting to show any weakness. I think of Jeremy, his cropped hair is different from not-my-roommate's head mop. Even the deepness of their brown eyes varies in the light, where Jeremy's brighten, this guy's consume.

"Julius, is this your idea of trying to set me up? I must tell you, I wasn't disappointed, but next time I prefer blondes." Blondes? Is he serious?

He interrupts Julius, who hunches over the desk where we left him earlier. Julius peers around his papers and mutters something into the receiver on his desk. He hangs up.

"Is there a problem?" Julius looks down at the box and then at the boy beside me. He lifts an eyebrow. "Did she carry that all the way down here?" His face is a mask of disappointment, but he manages to sound somewhat impressed. His lips press together and he swivels in his chair before he rises to his feet. He grabs the box from me and my joints protest with the ache of demanded relief. I stare at my fingers as I stretch them, flipping over my palm to catch the view of the other side. Not-my-roommate watches me.

"She wanted to carry it." He shrugs and my jaw clenches.

"Calix," Julius chides, clucking his tongue. He offers me an apology, but I don't hear it. *Calix*... His name is Calix. "Isabelle, I'll have you another room in a few minutes—this is my mistake." He sets the box on his desk and rushes back to his papers, reading over lists until he finds a chart.

"Isabelle," Calix whispers. I glance over at him, but he's staring down the stone-lined tunnel. My name an echo on his lips.

"Okay, here we go. Different floor, same number. I see the confusion now." Julius slides the key into my hand and smiles. "A little farther from Onyx, but I'm sure it'll do. Calix can show you where it is while I finish up what I'm doing here." Julius drops his chin to look at Calix as if he expects him to object. Calix's expression remains blank. "I'm trying to train him into the perfect gentleman, believe me, but this is ten years of progress." I glance at Calix with my mouth open, his eyes widen and he blinks. His face is solid and his expression grave, carved like a slab of stone. Ten years? "You have five minutes until dinner, I'm sorry you won't have much time to unpack." Julius pushes the box against Calix's chest and tucks in his chair with a kick.

"I got it." I grab it from him and strut through the familiar hallway I took earlier with Onyx.

"You sure?" I don't turn to see his expression or if he plans to follow.

"I carried it down here by myself, didn't I?"

This time my room feels more feminine. The walls are draped with posters of good-looking men I recognize from Brett's country phase. Luke Bryan, Jake Owen and Kip Moore all smile down with straight teeth over their guitars. Photocopied signatures stick to the bottom corners. I muse at the twin bed covered with pink plaid sheets. The fear of having a boring roommate evaporates from my mind the moment I slam the door on Calix.

I toss the box on my bed, emptying out its remnants. I know I don't have time to put them away, but at least now it's harder for the next person to kick me out. I shuffle towards the hallway and stop to lock the door as I watched Calix do earlier.

When I reach the front desk Onyx is leaning against the wall on the opposite side of the room. She examines the heel of her electric-blue stiletto. I round the corner, my apology ready on my lips, but it disappears at the sound of someone else's voice.

"Hey, Isabelle, is your new room more accommodating?" I twitch, startled by the unexpected greeting. Julius smiles and I can tell he's amused by the image of me, a new Descendant, finding Calix, an intimidating non-female, in my room.

"Much." I return his sincerity with a nod and Onyx watches.

When I reach her side she grips my wrist and steers us out the door. "How did you get a room change? I may need pointers for later." I laugh and shake my head.

"Technically it was never my room. I'm a floor under you now." I shrug and she's about to ask me to explain, but her eyes widen and her footsteps stutter. I follow her stare and I'm certain my expression mirrors hers.

"Shit, now we're never gonna find a seat." She rolls her eyes and grunts, already pushing past people as she goes.

The Meeting Square is crowded with rows of tables, the same ones that were hoisted up earlier on the patch of brown grass. Descendants hover over platters of food and I am stunned to find it's a buffet rather than portioned meals. Everyone packs together at random, grabbing any free spot they come across. Onyx arches her neck and balances on her toes, searching for Ash.

"Maybe we should grab a spot and he'll find us later. Two is easier to find than one." I suggest. We shuffle between people, some talking over what they saw in their exercises others wondering who the newcomers are. Everyone seems to know each other.

Someone pokes my shoulder and I whirl around to find a full head of blond curls. Her blue eyes sparkle with excitement. "You're a new face." She smiles and I find some reassurance that her front teeth curve inward.

"What's it to you?" Onyx stands beside me stiffly and I can only describe her stance as someone who has another's flank.

"My roommate was Summoned last year, that leaves me as a candidate to room with." She almost jumps with joy as she claps.

"Summoned?" I frown at Onyx for explanation and she waves me off.

"And you automatically think you're lucky enough to have one of us as your roommate?" Onyx rolls her eyes and the girl's cheeks drop.

"No, I know it. I asked Zilla. I got lonely." Her voice wavers and for a moment she looks sad. "I asked Julius for the name just a moment ago, right after class. You're Isabelle, right?" She asks, her words slow. I notice her Southern drawl. Jake Owen's smile flashes in my mind. If life were a cartoon, a lightbulb would go off above my head right now.

"How'd you know?" I ask. Onyx watches the stranger through narrowed lids and pursed lips.

"It's easy to spot the recruited. And you not knowing what a Summoning is kind of helped." Her freckled nose scrunches as she giggles a bubbly laugh.

"What is a Summoning?" I look at Onyx and back to the girl in front of me.

"It takes place at every year's end. Some Descendants get Summoned to work for the camp based on their balance or affinities." Onyx says through tight lips.

"Yeah, pretty much," the girl chirps in agreement. "Anyway, I'm Cattia." She beams.

"Oh great, and here I worried you'd have a hard name." Onyx glares and Cattia's brows lift together in confusion, not understanding her sarcasm.

She points at a table. "You can come sit with us. Ash is already waiting for you there. I'm sure your roommate will find you soon."

"I hope not," Onyx says and Cattia watches her from underneath scrunched brows. Onyx dashes around her, bumping against her shoulder in what could have passed as an accident. She aims for Ash who sits between two girls with waist-length black hair. Not like he notices as he scrapes his fork against his empty plate.

"Don't mind her. She takes some getting used to." I smile to Cattia, but she's watching the flame of Onyx's hair as it rounds the table.

Onyx's dark eyes absorb the blackness of Ash's hair as she prowls behind the group. She pinches his collar, plucking Ash from his seat in a swift movement that causes him to plop backwards off the bench. He lays on the sand stunned. Onyx shrugs, hitches a heel over him and nestles in the empty spot between the two girls. Ash rubs his neck and wipes the sand off his jeans. He scrutinizes the wooden table, trying to calculate what he did wrong.

Cattia chews on her bottom lip. "Is it rude to say that I'm happy you are Isabelle?"

I laugh. "Not at all." I make my way towards the table, trying hard not to examine the crowd of Descendants around me for a mop of black hair. I watch the ground send up puffs of dust around my new runners. Maybe clean clothes isn't something to get used to in a place covered in sand.

I sit across from two girls with black hair and the empty seat that was Ash's, and afterwards, Onyx's. She pulls him to the side and they whisper with their heads bent together. I watch them from the table of gushing girls.

"He's so cute, though."

"And he keeps looking over here."

"Oh my gosh, he's coming this way."

"Cattia!"

Someone clears their throat behind me and I break my gaze away from Onyx, but not before I catch her jaw slack. I swerve around to find Calix staring down at me. His deep brown eyes stealing whatever realization I am about to make.

My throat feels dry and I swallow. "You left this in my room." He presses something in my palm in a way that conceals it from everyone else's view. The girls lean over the table to sneak a peek at what it is. The weight of my phone feels heavy in my hand. How didn't I notice I forgot it? His voice drops and I know it's partially for show. "I'll have you know, if I were anyone else, I would have gone through it."

"How do I know you didn't?" I rise up from my spot. I drink in his height. My head would fit in the nook under his stubble-clouded chin. He tenses as if sensing the thought.

"I guess you'll have to trust me." His smug smile is back and I realize how close I am to his lips.

"My roommate is blonde in case you're interested," I blurt, feeling the weight of my tongue as I say it. My mouth fills with saliva and it tastes like bile.

He leans to look around me at Cattia, who stares at him with a dimpled grin and mock innocence. He makes a show of winking and I watch as the colour fills her cheeks. "I may take you up on that."

I roll my eyes and clutch my phone to my chest, gripping the screen harder.

He smirks and ducks his head. Strands of dark hair fall in front of his eyes. "I'll see you around, Isabelle." He says my name like a whisper and when I'm standing alone and he's no longer within view, I turn to face the goggling girls behind me.

"You're adjusting well," Onyx says, hovering next to me with her arms crossed over her chest. She nods her chin in the direction behind me and I know she means Calix. The two black-haired girls stare after him and Cattia narrows her eyes slightly towards me. Her lips purse as she concentrates on decoding the connection I might have to him.

"I remember when I first came here, I didn't want to talk to anyone. Do you remember that, Rachel?" One of the girls whirls to admire her lookalike. She whips her straightened black hair over her shoulder to mirror Rachel's.

"Yeah, you wouldn't leave our room. Now I can't seem to get you to shut up or come home." Rachel laughs and they huddle together gushing, reliving their first days and memories of how the first girl denied balance and called it a "social diet".

"It'll catch up to you. You'll get homesick and your new roomy here will have to comfort you." Onyx drapes an arm around Cattia's shoulder and her blonde curls are crushed under its weight. She cowers under Onyx's height and presses her lips together to avoid appearing frail.

"I don't have anyone to miss." I shrug.

"What do you mean?" Ash steps forward. The two girls fall silent and I can feel their stare on me. I toe the sand at my feet, sculpting tiny piles before I smooth them out again.

"Well, I have my sister and Jeremy, but they're at another camp." I glance up from under thick black lashes and catch Onyx chewing her lip. She knows the lie I feed myself to make their absence more bearable. "But I don't have a father—he left us when my mom died. I guess there's Aunt Jo, but I think she took us in because her cat made poor conversation." I shrug again and this time my shoulders feel heavy.

I hold my head high, breaking eye contact with the sand hill at my feet. Onyx's presses her ruby lips together in a thin line. I meet the stares of everyone at the table and nod. Ash touches my arm then reaches to pull his girlfriend onto the wooden bench next to him. He leaves a space and Cattia pats it for me to sit. Rachel talks to her roommate in a hushed voice and I know the introductions are done for the evening.

"Well, tomorrow you get your schedule, so that's exciting," Cattia says, trying to lighten the mood and I smile, but it doesn't reach my cheeks.

Chapter 10

I open my eyes to the view of a grey stone roof. A loud hammering wakes me. I groan and roll over. The spring of my mattress digs into my spine. Bony knuckles rap against the wooden door, leaving hollow echoes throughout the room. I jolt upward.

The image of Aunt Jo's white walls flashes through my mind before I realize where I am. The boxes piled on the floor will never find a home, displaced like Brett and me the past four months. Cans of orange paint are a failed attempt at a fresh start, abandoned like my sister. Twin beds were a frequent complaint, but now one is swapped for a new roommate.

I turn to ask Cattia who might knock on our door and find her pyjamas folded in a neat pile on her pillow. Her pink plaid sheets are tucked tightly under the mattress. I feel embarrassed that I wasn't awake to see her off. I stumble out of bed, not caring to fix the meadow green duvet Onyx pulled out of a bin last night. I fumble with the hem of my oversized T-shirt. The length covers my shorts, leaving my bare legs exposed. I dig through the heap of fabric on my floor to find pants. The knocking grows impatient.

I yank the silver knob and discover Zilla in the hall. She smiles her feral grin and if she's bothered by my unmade bed, she doesn't say. "Good morning." She nods and this time her smirk carries humour. I definitely slept in. "Your schedule is ready. Calix has offered to escort you to your first exercise. It takes place in Doctrine. You will find reassurance that your classes in Ordnance have a few familiar faces."

"Calix?" I echo.

Her grin is patient as she gestures down the hall. My mouth feels dry. I peep around the doorframe to find Calix leaning against the wall. He waves tauntingly. Black hairs fall in front of his eyes. I grip the hem of my shirt and try to tug it lower. "I hear you've met. I assure you, Calix is one of our most commendable Descendants." She clasps her hands and waits for an objection; when I don't give one, she nods. "I'll let you get ready. You are to meet in the Square in exactly eight minutes." She says no more as she veers down the hall, her oil-slick coat glides around her heels.

I close the door behind me, not caring if Calix is left alone. Commendable? I guess he has good aim. The image of his arrow striking against the chest of a waxwork dummy thuds in my mind and I shudder. I crouch down to the pile of clothes by my bed. I remind myself to put them away before Cattia files for a new roommate. I settle for one of the shirts Onyx picked and wiggle it over my head. My exposed cleavage makes me uncomfortable, but when I catch a glimpse of the time on Cattia's horse-framed clock, I realize it's too late to make an outfit change. I shove my arms into my old cardigan and fold it over myself as I trail out the door.

My new running shoes are filled with sand by the time I reach the centre of the Meeting Square. I drag my feet to Calix. His eyes linger on my chest and when I wrap my cardigan tighter around myself he turns away towards the towers of Doctrine. He's too far but I'm sure I catch the slight discolouring of his pale cheeks.

"Isabelle." He doesn't look at me. Man, what a jerk.

"Don't you have exercises you're enrolled in right now?" I approach Calix, silently warning myself to keep my distance.

He shrugs, scanning the distant tree line. Branches on the short oak trees sway in the breeze, their height stunted by the trunks of the towering evergreens. I muse at the assortment and can only imagine Jeremy's lecture on afforestation and required steps for saving the planet.

"You have Sight and Touch today. I'm doing this as a favour to Zilla." His voice sounds empty, cutting sharp edges around each word and reminding me once more that I should keep my distance. I linger behind until he's a few strides ahead. He glances over his shoulder and I can't tell if he smiles. I smirk and he turns away.

He didn't answer my question. "Are you going to come in my classes?" I prompt, raising an eyebrow though he can't see.

He chuckles and my feet stutter. I scan the ground to see if there's anything that would have made me stumble. Patted down dirt and misplaced footing mock me. "What makes you think I'd stay for beginner classes?" His words are harsh.

"What makes you think I need your guidance? Tell Zilla I got there safely, you're released from your burden." I shove past him and aim for the centre door. I rush around the corner quickly and lengthen my strides until I reach the familiar stone stairs at the East Wing. I take the steps two at a time and I realize no one told me which exercise I had first. I'm moving too fast to consider if I'm wrong. I count three halls and wheel into the centre aisle, the beginner's hall. There's a carved door on each side and I decide to pop into the closest. Descendants getting lost on the first day isn't exactly unheard of. I hope.

I peek around the corner. I don't know what I expected, but a room of five people doesn't seem to meet my standards. I guess there aren't any recently recruited.

"May I help you?" The wooden desks are arranged in a circle where the others frame the room, stacked up like barricades. The ages seem to vary as I examine the faces around me. The two boys with jet black hair could pass as siblings where the three girls share no resemblance in appearance. The eldest-looking smiles at me, her long black curls radiate youth where her laugh lines consume it. I realize she's the one who spoke.

"I came here for Sight." I swallow, even though the room is small my voice doesn't seem to carry. "Isabelle Lofflin,"

She nods, her smile spreads wide like her arms. "Welcome." She points to the boy next to her. "Dylan, get her down a seat and make room." He's about to object but thinks better of it, snapping his mouth shut and mumbling curse words as he pushes free from his desk.

"I could have gotten it," I offer. He lifts the legs above his head and throws it against the floor. It clatters and scrapes the tiles and I shudder. I reach for the chair, but he cuts off my path and nudges past me.

"There's no need, dear." Her joy seems permanent, never faltering as she speaks. "My name is Janet, we don't use last names here." She looks at the youngest of the two girls who stares down at her toes.

The girl mutters, "If we have hierarchy then power is lost amongst the ranks. We distribute it evenly if we plan to conquer." She recites the quote of a lecture she has drilled into memory.

"Good job, Ashna," Janet says. I observe everyone else, wondering if these Descendants are newly recruited or they were stuck, never advancing to the next level of Sight. No one explained how well you have to do in order to achieve more balance. Were there units, tests, end-of-the-year report cards? I stare at my desk now part of a conversing circle where the teacher is mixed among the classmates.

"Razielle, would you like to lead our discussion on Sight today? Summarize to Isabelle the most important aspect of the Sense." Janet waves to a girl with copper hair. Onyx would tease the poor dye job. Razielle shimmies her chair closer into the desk and sits straighter.

She comes at me animatedly, sounding over-ecstatic as if she finds this the most interesting fact in the world. Her eyes grow big and her hands start to play a leading role to her words as they swing, sway, and swoosh through the air. "You have to weed out the bullshit. Know when someone is pure and how to tell when the darkness is growing." Her fist thuds against her open palm. "It's not obvious, though. You don't know when someone has gone rogue by seeing them. We talked about this yesterday, sometimes a person can be fully converted and their family can't even tell. They're a walking parasite in society." She flails her arms around and I watch her through wide eyes.

"Parasite?" I echo.

"Yeah, sometimes demons use bodies as hosts. They want regular lives. It's actually the most common case." Razielle goes on to explain how to notice when a demon uses a body as a host, certain traits to search for, how the darkness grows slowly and becomes a part of the mind. "They twitch a lot and never make eye contact, that's the most obvious, but people usually think it's a nervous habit. The most noticeable to a person who genuinely knows the victim is when there's a change in routine, but most parents think of it as a rebellious stage or puberty." Razielle continues on about enlarged pupils and how in some cases the slurring of words is common.

How many people have I met on the streets that were developing darkness, how many people didn't know they needed help? My stomach knots and I pray silently that my sister and Jeremy are safe somewhere on a reserve, obtaining knowledge and belittling the chances of becoming a parasite.

I don't realize when Razielle stops talking or when Janet starts, but I follow as everyone starts tucking in their chairs and emptying out of the room. I watch the brown stone floor as I aim for the stairs. I brush my shoulder against a wall as I shuffle. Its cold surface keeps me alert and upright instead of bumping into passing shadows. I tiptoe down the stairs, a scene from *The Exorcist* playing over in my memory as I make my way to the centre hall of Touch.

Chapter 11

Beginners class for Touch is more crowded than Sight. I don't receive an introduction and the lesson picks up from yesterday.

"Sight is the most important thing you can have when fending off a demon. To see it is to know its power, its existence, to know it is different from you," someone says at the front of the sandy brick room. She hides behind a leather-bound notebook. All I can make out is the light brown hair that peeps above the delicate, thin pages. It's the kind of brown hair that suggests she was born a blonde. Her narrow fingers clutch at the frame of the cover. The bones of her knuckles stretch the pale skin of her hands and make her navy chipped nail polish seem less grunge-chic and more like someone your mom pulls you away from on the street. Two girls in front of her bicker about whether a shield is more important than a weapon.

"Hey, Cattia's roommate! Over here!" someone hisses and I whirl around, already walking away from Miss Punk to the promising stranger.

I recognize her black hair from last night. Rachel's roommate. I glance back at the girl carrying the leather notebook, down at my empty hands, then up at the pencil-covered desk she waves me to. My other lesson was only a discussion, I didn't notice any note takers. Leave it to Onyx not to pick me out any school supplies, but four different shampoos.

The desks are arranged in aisles, which made me falsely believe there would be a clear route to a seat. Instead, I sashay around pushed out chairs and tiptoe around hanging backpacks so I don't have to politely ask anyone to tuck in.

"Thank God I know someone. This Sense was just starting to get boring." She flips her hair and bites the cap of her pen. "I'm Lara, by the way." She winks an eyelid full of dark curled lashes.

"Isabelle," I say. "Are you new, too?"

Lara snorts. "Nope, I've been here two years. Came right off the train with Rachel in case you were wondering about my brain sister." Her green eyes stare at me from under a row of straight front bangs.

"Brain sister?" I echo. Surely that's not more lingo I have to define in my personal dictionary. "You have a shared affinity?"

She snorts again. "It's an ongoing joke we have. You'll catch on when we're together." She shrugs and doodles on the wood of the desk. "To answer your question, no, I'm not a beginner. I'm weak in Touch. Not enough to move to a different camp, though. When I first arrived I sucked at Sight more. The recruited are generally sent here." I think of Crystal and how she defined Touch when gesturing to Brett. *They do not know when to apply effort singularly because they split it amongst many things.* The weight of my cell phone feels heavier.

"Well, I'm glad I know someone." I rack my brain for something else that sounds like a normal response.

"*Guarde su alivio. Hay más peligro aquí,*" Lara mutters, her R's roll effortlessly and I'm miffed by how easily she can swap between Spanish and English. "This is my only class without her," she continues.

"Who?"

"Rachel," she scoffs. "Who else?" She arches a thinly plucked brow.

"Lara?" A male voice calls from the front of the room. A slim figure leans against the wall away from the crowd of unbalanced Descendants. "Care to answer...?" He looks at someone sitting in front of him.

"Jonathan," the boy says.

"Yes, care to answer Jonathan's question?"

She purses her lips and rests her head on her intertwined fingers. "Repeat it?" She blinks too many times in a second. The instructor straightens his glasses and squints in her direction. She licks her lips.

"What is the most obvious use of Force?" he says, repeating the unheard question.

"Beat the crap out of someone?" Her Spanish accent drops in tone, creating seduction in her uncertainty, tempting him to tell her she's wrong and craving the challenge.

"In a way, yes, that is right. However, Touch can also relate to Voice, where the force of leading and persuasion holds power. Touch focuses more on combat, your strengths and how you overcome obstacles. You will see more of these exercises in Ordnance." He spins on his heels and marches up and down the front aisle. Lara bites at her lip. "The easiest way to get lost in Force is by trying to save everyone. You can't act as the hero. Can anyone elaborate?" He points to the girl with the leather-bound book. She places it down, revealing pixie-short hair and the slim angle of her jaw.

"You try to apply yourself to everything. To save everyone rather than picking the most important thing to conquer." She appears bored when she speaks. "Often, someone tries to save the person from the demon instead of realizing they're no longer separate entities and killing it. The mistake is commonly done when facing family."

I shiver. If it were Brett or Jeremy at risk, could I kill them? I'd try to save them. I'd make the mistake of thinking they could surface above the demon. I'm not strong enough to fend off the body of someone I love. I couldn't mark the skin of someone I hold when I feel fear, even if they cause it.

This is why I'm a beginner.

I imagine Brett's frail body, her fists clenched at her side and a look in her blue eyes that always challenges someone to move against her. She'd climb thin trees in the summertime to prove feeble limbs can carry greater weight. Her nails are always dirty from taking apart her bike and assembling it to its previous condition. I imagine my mom rolling the same blue eyes at the pair of grass-stained shoes she bought Brett a day ago. Brett always searches for adventure and she never needs a partner or a protector. She does fine on her own.

My sister, unlike me, is headstrong. She has to fix everything and if she struggles the only display of weakness she allows is a grunt of frustration. I have to believe that if she overcomes camp she'd become one hell of a warrior. I've seen her determination in many things and can imagine her Force if she places it in one.

"Unfortunately we're getting tight on time. For when you find yourself a spare moment, I want you to go to the arena and find a weapon of choice. You have until next week to report your decision to me. We will review ways in which they are beneficial in fending off certain demons." He turns away from the class to conclude his lesson.

"I already know what I'm gonna bring in. A shield is obviously the best option." A girl steps in front of us, carrying on her rant about the importance of defence.

"Suit yourself. I'm going to show up with the sharpest axe I can find." Her friend joins in.

The two girls continue their argument as they exit the room. I look at Lara and she covers her mouth hiding her laughter. "If you come back with a shield, I will personally show you how it can be used as a weapon." She swings her arms at me clutching an invisible board. I laugh and try to dodge it.

She nudges my shoulder. "C'mon, chica, let's go get some lunch."

Chapter 12

By the time Lara finally stops talking to every person we bump into, I'm able to spot Onyx and Ash leaving their table. Her red hair whips as she turns to see who calls her name. Her black eyes widen and she clutches onto Ash's arm steering their tall bodies towards me.

"Yeesh, any later? Start eating before you lose a bra size." She nudges me against a wooden bench and I reach for a mangled olive vine on the table. I glance over my shoulder and find Lara engaged in another intense discussion about how she'd fail Touch again just to stare at Oliver's *caliente* ass. I assume that's our instructor.

"Your exercises in Ordnance should line up with Doctrine. So we have Sight then Touch." Onyx says, reaching her long arm across the table to grab an empty plate then fills it with vegetables before she shoves it towards me. "I'm guessing you only like rabbit food?" I reach for a carrot and make a show of biting it. It crunches and Onyx rolls her eyes.

"You said we," I note. I watch her face as she lowers it. Her ruby lips spread and if I didn't know her humour I would be terrified.

"What, a familiar friend on your first day isn't anything to feel thankful for?" Onyx imitates doe eyes. I laugh and push aside my plate reaching for more olives. She wrinkles her nose.

"What?" I pop another in my mouth and swap it for a shaved seed between my fingertips.

"How do you eat those?" Her nose wrinkles again and her eyes watch as I place another seed onto my plate.

"What, you don't like olives?" Now my nose scrunches. I can eat a whole jar.

"Are you done? You're running late," Ash says from behind Onyx.

"What do you mean, you're not coming?" I wait for Onyx's explanation. She stares at my olive seeds.

"I have to go, sweetheart." He kisses Onyx on the cheek and struts off. Her eyes don't leave my plate.

"Okay, time to go, Big Boobed Bertha." She stands up and brushes off her jeans. Her black strappy heels make her a head taller than me. I'm about to ask where Ash is going, but Onyx's eyes widen. I follow her view and find Julius, leaning against the Residence building. A grin stretches across his cheeks. I attempt to wave, but Onyx is too quick. She grabs my wrist and pulls me towards Ordnance. This time dirt doesn't kick up around my feet as they drag long, wiggled lines behind me.

I peer through squinted lids and catch her black heels walk through the hollowed stone doorway. Onyx bows towards our Sight instructor, a lady whose wardrobe consists of different shades of grey. Onyx receives a nod and goes on to enthuse a grand royal wave until she is no longer in view.

We're supposed to meditate, find our inner Knowledge or whatever. Sounds like a breeze, until you're told to sit on the stone floor and nothing else. No other instructions were said and I don't want to ask. Freedom is granted the longer you sit still without fussing. I think.

I squeeze my eyes shut to make the images appear again. Crystal waving her arms in a wall of smoke, the clouds forming images of hooves and a train. Brett waking up that morning I promised her we would go to communicate with Mom. Jeremy wearing a black tux and holding flowers. Aunt Jo peering behind curtains. Mom's smile. My father's suitcase. Dark eyes. A sharp nose and a sarcastic smirk. I glance around the room.

No clock is visible on the wall but my sore limbs tell me I've been sitting here a long time.

"Concentrate, Isabelle. You will not find peace in yourself if you are not content with the image of nothing." The instructors voice echoes somewhere in the distance and I try to figure out if she's more to my left or right.

I'm the last one stuck in here. I sit up a little straighter and inhale deeply trying to calm my thoughts once more.

My fingers start to twitch. I realize the voice inside my head telling everything to shut up deducts from the silence within my own mind. I exhale slowly and let myself submerge in the pictures of my family. I figure they can't keep me here all night. It's a split second later when I realize they can.

Crystal. Brett. Jeremy. Aunt Jo. Mom. Dad. Dark brown eyes that can pass as black. I let them consume me like a void, hoping they will take me into nothing and silence the voice in my head that wakes up everything. My breathing shallows and my muscles loosen. My mind releases and the tension diminishes like a blown out flame, but instead of feeling cold I'm warm. My veins burn and I can feel the blood course through my body. Each pore prickles against the light breeze in the room. My blood ignites, sparks shine behind my lids like a live wire. My sore limbs wake and my tailbone flexes straight. The darkness allows me to notice the light that grows within my body. I smirk at the irony. To submerge myself in nothing, but to see everything.

"You may go."

The brown eyes blink and mine open. "That's it? You want me to sit still for ten seconds?"

"It has been an hour." She walks away from me towards the stone arch doorway. An hour all together, or an hour with my eyes shut? "And if you think what you experienced is sitting still, then perhaps you need more lessons." She gives me a pointed look and watches as I scramble to my feet. She calls over her shoulder, "If you remain ignorant, you are not protecting your mind, you're destroying it." She leaves.

I rush to follow her into the hall, but she disappears into the shadows. So that's why she chooses such a colourless wardrobe.

Chapter 13

"Are you trying to starve yourself because so far you've tried to opt out of every meal time." Onyx glares up at me from the wooden bench.

"I just finished in Ordnance." I groan, plop down beside her and rest my elbows on the table, jamming my palms into my eyes. The dark void stares at me. I shake my head, hoping memories erase like an Etch A Sketch.

"So are you hoarding food in your room or what?" Onyx pokes me. Across the table, Cattia scrunches her nose, not enjoying the idea of snacks being stashed in our room.

"No," I answer. "But I wish I had some of Aunt Jo's homemade mac-and-cheese leftovers right now." An image of gooey noodles stuck together by strands of melted cheese makes my mouth water. They always taste better the next day.

"Here, have some ribs. It's kind of the same thing." Onyx places a rack of bones with sauced meat on the plate in front of me.

"How is that the same?" I drop my arms.

"Close enough." She shrugs. "I think you have a fear of meat on bones." She grabs my wrist and dangles it in front of me to show how her fingers loop around with ease. I chomp down a big bite of a rib and chew with my mouth open. I don't mention how it tastes dry or the thickness of my thighs, but

I must have impressed her because she smiles and nods with approval. "Atta, girl."

"So, how did you get out of Sight so quickly?" I watch Onyx as she rests into Ash's side. I'm about to ask if she saw the same dark eyes, but if I have learned anything so far it's that no one sees the same thing.

"I guess the reserve taught us a few things. It was like meditating. You have to listen to your blood." She grabs my plate and throws on some steamed vegetables and potatoes.

"What happens if I miss a lesson?" By the time I left Sight it was already dinner time and I didn't make it to Touch.

"It's not like that. Every day is a lesson. You don't need to know the previous day to work on the next. They're all different strategies that test your Sense."

"What did you do in Touch?" I lean closer, a little jealous that I didn't get to witness it myself.

"I pretty much watched Cattia drool the whole time." Onyx drags a sharp nail from the corner of her mouth to her chin, drawing an invisible line of spit.

Cattia looks away. Her face matches the red pepper I stab with my fork. Her fingers shake as she reaches for her napkin and she dabs her already dry lips. "I'm unsure what you mean." She tries to meet Onyx's eyes, but her focus is on the table. I quickly grew used to Onyx's attitude, but something tells me Cattia's Southern hospitality can't relate.

Onyx imitates the display of Cattia daydreaming with doe eyes up at the sky. "You were completely checked out." Onyx clasps her hands under her chin and flutters her eyelashes. Cattia's jaw clenches.

"He walked up to me and offered to show me how to shoot." Cattia crosses her arms. Shoot. A crossbow? I stare at her blonde hair as the wind sweeps some curls away from her face. Calix offered?

"Hear that Izzy? Your friend over there is a good Samaritan." She nods in the direction past the table and I spin on the bench.

Calix leans against the door of Ordnance. With the sun setting, the Meeting Square is cast in the shadow of Doctrine making it hard to decipher his expression underneath the veil of darkness. I try to read the shadows of his eyes and even from across the field I know he's smirking.

A screech pierces through the Meeting Square and echoes off the buildings.

People stand, racing to join an already formed huddle. They crowd together, creating a wall of bodies so I can't see in. At first I thought the group came together out of curiosity, but they create a barrier to cage in the thing at the centre of the circle. The table seats are empty as Descendants work together to hold in the threat.

I envy Onyx's heel choice as I reach on my toes for a better view. Cattia somehow made it as part of the barrier, but she gasps and gives up her spot to the next person in line. Lara rushes forward and fills the gap, but not before I catch a glimpse.

The boy in our Touch class, Jonathan, withers on the floor. The four Preceptors take their spots within the circle, equally spaced out like a compass. Zilla positions herself at the North and Caradoc at the South. Jonathan pukes and red smears his grey skin. Blood. It pours from his eyes and his nose, spotting his striped green-and-blue shirt. He sits sweaty, hunched over and twitching. His veins protrude and his lips pale.

I search for more glimpses of Jonathan through the legs of the people around him. I want to reach on my tiptoes or crouch lower, but I stand still, the farthest body from the group.

An arm clenches around my elbow and tugs me away. At first I let it, too numb to lift my feet and my brain too stuck on the image in front of me. My mind wakes up and my muscles tighten. I swing a fist at the person behind me. Prepared to kick at some shins and bite a limb if I have to.

"What the fuck, stop!" Calix growls. He flexes a forearm in front of him to defend my clawing nails.

"Why are you grabbing me!" I shout.

"You don't want to see that." He touches a loose strand of my black hair and lets it twirl around his finger before he drops it. His dark brown eyes sneer down at me.

"How would you know? Looks like it's starting to get good." I cross my arms.

"They're going to kill him." Calix lowers his chin to study me. My jaw locks, my eyes stare, and I try to stand fearless, composed like a Descendant—who recently found out she has angel blood in her system and that there's a slight probability a demon could take over her body—should be. He smirks, but this time his eyes are soft. "Train and that won't happen to you."

"Or you're going to have to kill me yourself? Or maybe Cattia since I heard she's been training her shot." I lift my chin to appear taller. His breath brushes against my face and I have the urge to flinch. He smirks. His eyes blend into the shadows of Doctrine.

"Take care of yourself, Belle."

Luke Bryan stares at me from across the room. Cattia's annoying horse clock ticks with every second that passes. Brett and Jeremy have to be safe, but as I think of Calix's warning it reminds me that I may not be, either. My blood can reject the Sight even while I'm here.

I fluff my pillow and fumble my fingers against the mattress until I feel the cool surface of my phone. The screen lights up and I shimmy deeper into my sheets to hide the glare. The lump of covers in Cattia's bed doesn't move. I wait for a lull in her breathing and when there isn't one I sit up. It is past midnight and I can't sleep.

I swing my legs off the bed and grab a shirt from the floor. I make a mental promise to myself that I will find a place for my new belongings before Cattia complains. A pair of grey training pants tease me from the bottom of the folded load. I tug at them and the pile topples over. The deed is done. No use crying over spilt laundry. I pull sweatpants up from my ankles and tie the string around my waist. I kick my flip-flops under the bed and swap them for a pair of runners.

I hold the knob as I swing the door closed. It shuts behind me with a soft click. I face the hallway. Closed doors dash the walls and line the length of the building. Dim yellow bulbs mark the stoned ceiling. There's no windows to distinguish that I'm above ground. My laces tap as I jog down the hall.

Chapter 14

Fresh air hits the sweat on my chest. I sprint across the empty Meeting Square. The tables are pushed to the side for the night and will be rearranged to line the lot for breakfast in a few hours.

Sand collects in my shoes and slides under my socks, filtering through the fabric to my toes like an hourglass. I glance around the empty sand Square and plan an alternate route through the tunnels of Doctrine for next time. I don't know how strict the curfew rules are, but I'm not about to stand in the middle of open space waiting to find out.

I have to make up for my missed lesson in Touch. I can't risk losing balance. I stroll through the dark L-shaped hallway, blind to all direction. I follow the memory of my tour. The steep stairs descend farther underground. The room opens up and bleachers line the walls. The gym is a hollow hole beneath the surface of the Ordnance lecture halls as if carved into the stone floor.

Equipment sits freely on tables and racks along the walls. I take it as a sign of welcome that nothing is locked up. Instructions and codes do not hang anywhere. As I step into the arena I realize I have no clue where to start.

A tunnel branches away from the centre of the arena and into a closet filled with dummies, blade sharpeners and a tub of murky water someone forgot to empty. Weapons of all weights and lengths hang along the circular wall. I recognize a few: spears, nunchucks, swords, batons, shields, axes, and daggers. Like walking into a twelve-year old boy's dream. Minus the women.

I drag a waxwork dummy into the centre of the gym, the immediate centre of the circular arena. I pace around the figure, studying its angles and how I can get the best shot. Without hesitation, I grab the smallest blade, ignoring the crossbow that sits beside it.

The arch of the handle fits comfortably in my palm. The blade narrows into a thin slit, creating an imbalance as the light weight of the tip resists against the heaviness of the handle. I swing the knife over my shoulder and then aim at the target. It clatters on the ground a meter in front of the dummy. I grab another off the wall, this time holstering two more in my weapon belt for later.

The blade pokes the waxwork shoulder and fumbles over, landing not far from another on the floor. I throw the last two. I miss both. I retrieve them from the ground.

I yell profanity and grunt non-specific sounds, throwing careless shots to satisfy my adrenaline. My clothes stick to me, restraining each hurl and providing me with something to blame. I crouch with my head on my knees for a bit. My hair falls in heavy waves down my back and I use the elastic from my wrist to restrain it. I stand up.

I imagine Brett eyeing the weapons on the wall and understanding their use by running her frail fingers over them. She would hit the heart within her first five swings. Jeremy wouldn't need a weapon with his body, but the image of him carrying a long spear seems fitting. I sneer at the dummy and pick up a knife to try again. I will not let down my family.

I feel the weight of the handle in comparison to the tip and toss the blade so the heavier side guides it, it meets the stomach with a thud then clatters to the floor. I pick the next one up and eye the centre of the chest again, another thud. I don't care that the blades don't stick and hold—I found my weapon for Touch.

Chapter 15

My arms refuse to cooperate with me all morning. My fingers forget how to clasp the slippery soap in the shower and the bar spends a lot of time at my feet. When I bend to grab my book bag, I swear I say bye to Cattia from eye level—my hunched back causing me to lose an inch and a half in height. I question whoever says pain after a workout feels good.

"Does it really cripple you that much to get out of bed on time for breakfast?" Onyx stares at me with raised eyebrows.

"I went to Ordnance last night." I groan as I fall onto a wooden bench where three hours ago would have been hard sand.

"You sure you didn't sneak out to meet someone?" Cattia takes a seat next to me.

"What?" I'm the first to ask, but the rest of the table falls quiet, swapping their attention from their food to my and Cattia's conversation.

"I woke up in the middle of the night and you weren't there." She shrugs and leaves the bench to signal Rachel and Lara over.

"You share a room with her. We know the blonde is real but what about the curls?" Onyx examines the back of Cattia's head. I nudge her arm. Ash walks over with a plate, his eyebrows scrunched together at the bell-like sound of Onyx's laughter.

I stare at the strips of meat on my plate that someone called turkey bacon. It tastes like plastic. I eat it before Onyx can tease me with pointers about breast size without proper fat intake. I twirl the fork and count my chews, but the meat doesn't break. I miss Aunt Jo's pancakes.

I reach for the syrup to follow the path of my brilliant plan—drown the bacon. My fingers are just shy of the brown, gooey liquid breakfast saviour, when a blade stabs Aunt Jemima's face. The bottle gulps the air until it empties. Syrup drenches the wooden table. I know I should show more concern for flying knives, but instead I worry about attracting a swarm of bees.

"What the heck?"

"Cattia, if you're going to swear do it right. Can you say fuck? Say it. *Fuh-uck.*" Onyx swings her pointer finger in the air to teach the table octaves.

Ten pairs of eyes stare at the bleeding Jemima. They all turn to me. I turn to the thrower.

Calix stands with his fists in his pocket. A smirk pinches his cheek.

I'm rising from the bench before I realize I'm about to confront someone who almost stabbed my hand and ruined my breakfast.

"What the fuck?" I say. Onyx would be proud.

"Just showing you how to sink a blade properly." He starts to walk away.

"By amputating my hand!" He doesn't answer. I follow him. His pace doesn't falter as I tug his shirt. I cut him off. The light cotton texture hugs the muscles of his chest. I tighten my grip and drag him after me. We enter Ordnance. "How did you even know?"

"Do you want to learn or not?" he says. He keeps his voice levelled as he stops to look at me. I examine the stubble on his chin and the hard line of his mouth. It's soft, full even. Does this place have ChapStick? I bite at the skin of my dry lips.

"Are we avoiding questions with more questions?" I lift my chin, but I still stand below his. He reaches for a strand of my hair but stops himself. The light flickers from a single bulb above us. I can feel the heat from his body and the cool air of his breath. Spearmint.

"I'll see you later, Belle." This time he doesn't hold back. He tugs a curl before he leaves. His footfalls are silent as he retreats farther into the dimly lit hallway.

I don't follow him.

"So. How was the make-out session?" Onyx leans into me out of earshot from Cattia, who hasn't looked away from me since I sat down.

"It's not like that. He threw a knife at me!" I hang my head, unable to bear the weight of my curls.

"Maybe that's just Meeting Square talk for he has a crush on you." Onyx picks at her ruby nail polish. Ash stares at her in disbelief. You would think he's immune to her craziness after dating her.

"Is anyone going to break the news and tell you that you are insane?" I push my plate away from me and Cattia looks away.

"The doctors have been telling me that for years."

A chime tells the crowd to break for lessons. Onyx stands, digging her purple suede wedges into the sand. She gives me the finger and smiles. She grabs Ash's sleeve and tugs him after her. He doesn't speak as he follows. They were almost through the clearing when Julius interrupts by placing a concealed letter in Onyx's palm. I squint through the passing people to get a better view. Julius' hand lingers on Onyx's for a moment and Ash lets go of her first. He bows to the Preceptor before turning away. Julius strolls towards Residence. Onyx struts behind him too gracefully for sand. Her jaw clenches, red hair bounces, and her fingers are in fists. Ash retreats into Ordnance without glancing back.

I stand from my seat not knowing if I should follow or make my way to Voice. I settle for heading to Doctrine; if I'm needed they'll find me. I promise myself I will ask Onyx about it later.

Voice exercises are how I would imagine a debate class to play out. Not the actual debate, but how to structure a winning argument. The classroom is set up like an auditorium with chairs circling a wooden podium. Descendants stand up and raise their voices and fists as if it will benefit their point. I remain seated the entire time.

Sound class takes place in the towers, which means there's actually windows and a view of outside. I pull up a seat next to one. The breeze is warm and the sun shines across the Square, highlighting a few lingering people. Are we allowed to skip lessons? I watch the trees and plot a potential escape.

"Concentrate on the wind. Close your eyes, Charlie." Someone grunts in response.

A soft patter of footsteps paces the front of the room. I squeeze my eyes shut.

"What do you feel?" Aliza whispers.

"Cold." I mumble. Someone nudges me.

Aliza continues to walk the length of the room. "Now, peers, this tower is a place to delve into the affinity of Sound. Open up to your senses. Inhale. Relax. Breathe." Heavy breathing and gasps fill the brick room on the fourth floor of Doctrine. The sunlight heats my eyelids.

I kick my feet under the desk, forming small tapping patterns. Aliza clears her throat and without peeking, I plant my feet, roll my neck and slouch.

I count down from thirty. I quiet my thoughts and clear away any distracting reminders, like what Onyx and Julius were talking about this morning. I number my breaths. Meditating has become a routine during the past few classes. Thoughts of Jeremy and Brett surface, but I push them away. I will save my dwelling for my bedtime. Maybe then my body will feel too tired to worry. I close myself to the lesson and imagine Jeremy and Brett at home, sitting on the wire love seat while Aunt Jo spies through the curtains. I'm at a summer camp and I will tell them all the bizarre stories I witness.

And then I hear it.

It pierces through the image in my head. Brett and Jeremy are gone. A tearing sound slices through the breeze and the wind whips through the tower. My shirt flutters and my hair catches in my lips. The room falls silent and the breathing hushes. I want to open my eyes but they're stuck shut. Does anyone hear it? The silence is split apart by a harsh cry and I can't place the words before the next gust muffles it. My heart races and my gut tells me to react, to run. It's urgent, it can't wait. What can't wait? The muffled mutters call out a message I can't decipher. A warning.

"What?" I whisper. "Tell me what you need."

No one replies.

The wind stops and everything falls still.

I strain my ears to catch the message again, hoping it will repeat.

A soft hum responds. It's the light harmony of the leaves singing. It's "The Song from the Trees" that we were told to listen for at the beginning of class.

No one is there.

"You may open your eyes," Aliza says. Her page ruffles and then smooths. I look around the room to see if anyone else has crazy-eyes. Bored faces mock me. "Did the sound come easier today?" This is an ongoing exercise at the end of every lesson.

"I didn't hear anything." A petite, fair-haired girl says from the back of the room. The guy at the front of the room hangs his spiked head in irritation and the girl across from me narrows her yellow eyes.

"I told you Mary-Anne, you're struggling because you are not focused. Have you been attending your meetings with Ash?" Mary-Anne hides behind her packed purse. Her forehead tints an awkward shade of pink. I think of Ash and his quiet arrogance. I could understand the lack of progress and undeniable fear Mary-Anne has.

I'll have to ask Ash how he scored a tutoring job. Another thing added to the list of unsolved questions.

"I heard a voice," I say before I register my lips moving. Mary-Anne glances up and smiles. Obviously glad for the diversion from her. Aliza raises her eyebrows and her lips part.

Someone snorts.

"Could have been Jerry's stomach." Charlie laughs. So does the rest of the room.

Instead of trying to gain control of the Descendants, Aliza dismisses us to lunch.

I find Ash on the way out.

Despite my constant prying, Ash's quick topic changes make it so that I never did find out why he sat in on my Sound lesson.

"'Sup Breast Nest. No wonder Calix took a liking to you. We saw his bed. He could use extra pillows." Onyx sits down next to me and Ash stands up to leave. She watches him, crumbling the crust of her sandwich. I pull my shirt up to my chin.

"Hey, Ash was in my Sound class. Does he not have his own lessons?" I nudge her. My poor attempt to change the topic away from my boobs.

"Oh. Uh. Yeah." She stares after him. Ash rushes into Residence and Mary-Anne shuffles to catch up next to him, trailing steps behind as she struggles to balance food on a paper plate. A carrot falls into the sand.

"So. What's with Julius?" Attempt number two.

"What do you mean?" Onyx demands. Her eyes switch between mine, waiting for an answer. Her red brows push together and she grabs my wrist. I drop my fork and the piece of turkey I saved for the last bite. The sand gobbles it up.

"He gave you a letter and you left to talk. What's it about?" I glance down to my fallen food, and Onyx releases my arm. She twists to the table and wears her regular sarcastic smile.

"Oh, that… It's nothing."

I sit and watch her bite into her crust-less sandwich.

"So. I think my boobs grew," I say.

Cattia asks more questions than Aunt Jo, which I never thought was possible. By the end of her inquiry she settles for giving me her back and ordering me to pick up my clothes off the floor. I don't know why she's upset, but it's late when I finish cleaning.

My runners carry the sand with each stride as I cross the Square. A light patter of footfalls cut through the silent clearing as I maintain my pace. I enter Ordnance and rush down the length of the L. The dull bulbs flicker as I pass, illuminating the walls but not the ground. I slow to a jog as I dive farther into the darkness, feeling for each step as the floor slopes down to the gym area. My eyes adjust and I aim for the fluorescent hue around the bend.

The bleachers circle the domed room and the familiar dirt of the Meeting Square carpets the stone training floor. I punch the waxwork dummy as I pass, a warning for later business. Thank God someone left it from a previous work out because grunting, windedness and the physical struggle to roll it out would ruin my bravado. I duck under the arched doorway of the equipment room and head to the knife wall. Under a white light, each blade glistens, held securely by individual stone hooks. I trail my finger over each weapon, comparing the shafts to my forearm, leg and head. The width varies as the wall stretches. Some are smooth, with a slick and polished curve of the blade, while others have razor-edged teeth. I scan for the small, familiar knife I used before and lift it from its hoist. I study the feel of the handle in my palm. I stab four more into my belt holster and face my target.

"Ready to learn, Belle?" Calix rests an arm around the shoulders of the dummy.

"What are you doing here?" I snarl. So maybe the waxwork wasn't here from a previous lesson, just an impatient stalker.

"I said I would see you later." He smirks. He cuts through the space between us with a confident strut and strides past me. I snort, readying a brilliant retort.

"Stand with your legs apart." He orders. I'm about to ask who invited him, but he kicks my ankle. The motion separates my right foot away from my left. I hiss, twisting my torso to scowl at him. He places his palms on my shoulders, spinning me around and forcing me forward. "Square yourself with your target." He curves my body, pointing a finger at the dummy as if I don't know where my target is. I roll my eyes. "Now, grip the knife so you are comfortable, but not too tight. Remember, you'll have to let it go. The movement should occur as a seamless transition." He steps in front of me. His fingers brush against mine and over the blade. I warm at his touch. His cool skin ignites something in mine and sends tendrils of electricity to my chest. My pulse quickens. His brown eyes are firm, not wavering as he gazes down at me. They're darker than mine by a few shades. They glint in the fluorescent light of the arena. A patch of black hair falls over his eyebrow and tickles his forehead. We stand, silent, waiting for the other to protest. His request for obedience will challenge my agility. And my patience. I cross my arms and fix him with a glare, tempting him to break contact first.

"Belle…" He breathes my name out in a huff of spearmint. He drops his chin, smirks, and then moves to stand behind me again. "I told you that you're going to have to trust me."

"I do." I whisper.

Silence.

"Relax. Straighten up." Calix places a palm on my stomach and another on my back. I close my eyes to avoid the feeling of his clammy palms and concentrate on the texture of the knife. I inhale and stretch my neck, arching my back with as much good posture as I can manage. Aunt Jo would be pleased.

"Now, bring the blade to eye level and focus on the target." I squint to inspect the chest of the dummy. "Practice the motion of the throw, see the path you want the blade to take." I flex my elbow, extending the blade away from my body and bringing it to my cheek. "You want to bend your torso forward when you throw not your elbow." Calix pushes my shoulders forward and up, bowing me towards the waxwork. "Place your right foot in front of the left, you want to step into the throw. Release when the tip is at the target."

I lunge forward, bowing my shoulders, releasing my grip, following the path I envisioned earlier. The blade thuds to the floor. I wait for Calix to laugh and tease me, demanding me to leave the arena, admit defeat and pray I don't die from imbalance. He slips another blade into my hand.

"Feel the weight of the knife to understand its movement. Get comfortable. You're focusing too hard on succeeding that you're missing the fluidity of the shot." I don't say anything, I grit my teeth, take another knife and throw. This time with nothing in mind, not even the target. It clatters somewhere between the rows of stone bleachers.

"Show me your hand." He reaches for my fingers. I jerk away, swinging my palm up to rest on my cheek.

I take a step and a deep breath. I move the sweaty curls from my forehead and reach for a hair tie. "I can do it." Alone. I don't say the last part.

"I know you can, I'm just showing you how." Calix grabs my fingers away my face and places them around the knife. "The handle is heavier so you want to use it to angle the force of the shot. Now, how you hold it can be different. You're gripping it with your entire hand, which can restrict the flow of your release. I would like you to try pinching the blade with your thumb and first knuckle." He moves my thumb to clasp the dagger. The knife rests against my first knuckle awkwardly. The blade feels flimsy and wobbles from my grip. He smirks and I scowl.

"I don't like this way." My brows pinch together. I hear the whine in my voice and snap my mouth shut. I sound like a stubborn child. In my defence, a child who refuses to play with knives is not a bad thing.

"Get comfortable with the motion, Belle. No one is expecting you to master it on your second time. Now, you can try throwing it horizontally like a frisbee, if you want." He lets go of a blade, just like that. It helicopters through the air and pierces the dummy in the neck. I gawk at the clear incision.

"Teach me how to do that and I promise it won't foreshadow your ironic death." I grab his wrists. He chuckles. A rumble of laughter vibrates deep in his chest. His smile reveals a row of straight teeth. I gawk. Before I could save the vision to memory his smirk returns. The tension releases from his cheeks and his eyes glint brighter.

"Sorry, darling, you will never have the opportunity to shoot straight when you're defending yourself. Your shots will have to be in motion. It's easy to aim straight when you're standing still, but I will accept your admiration and you may continue to fangirl me for the rest of your existence." I shove him and he pulls on my curls.

"Why need me, when you have Cattia?" I cross my arms and wait for his response.

"Oh, shut up." He steps closer to me. "You could take her once you master a spin throw." He watches me laugh, waiting for the next chorus to finish. It ends with a snort, sending him into fits of mimicked pig calls. For the first time since I arrived at camp I feel like myself.

"I don't really think I'll be fighting many bad guys in my days, but I'll remember that." I smile, but his is gone. His eyebrows pinch together and his lips form a straight line.

"You still don't believe you're here for a purpose, do you?" His expression is wiped clean from the evidence of earlier laughter. He clenches his fists and his breathing comes harsh.

"I—well. I'll leave eventually." I don't plan on staying here long. My mental checklist on what I need to do to get out of here goes as follows: attend exercises, practice, find balance, maybe develop an affinity, find Brett.

"Your ignorance will consume your Sight and the good in your blood." Calix struts across the arena towards the dummy.

"Don't you want to leave?" He stops. I reach for him. I want to force him to look at me, demand for me to stay. I wait. He doesn't move.

"I can, but I have nowhere to go." His voice is low.

"You can leave?" I place hesitant steps around him, certain that anything quicker would scare him away. I stand under his chin. His hair hangs loose and his eyes are shut. Dark lashes brush against the defined angle of his cheekbones.

"Yes." And that's all he says. The silence rings on and my questions grow. He's balanced? Well, he's been here for ten years, knows the Preceptors, can probably maneuver every weapon on the wall. It makes sense and yet, he still stays. I try to imagine that decision. Every day surrounded by the same people, watching them filter as some leave and some die. The buildings act as a rectangle perimeter to his existence.

"I have a sister. Her name is Brett. She's a pain in the ass, but she's all I have," I blurt, trying to justify my choice, rather than confront his. I think of Jeremy and Aunt Jo and feel guilty. They try so hard, and I love them. I know they will take care of my sister when I cannot and I know they'll do it for me. But Brett is my responsibility; she's a part of me and her eyes are the only living memory left of my mother.

"I need to leave so I can find her."

He opens his eyes. The black contracts back to the centre and the brown consumes me. It's a shade I haven't seen before, like dark chocolate or roasted chestnuts. Onyx would pride me for the food analogy. My lips twitch. He stares at them.

"You can't sneak me out?" I wiggle my eyebrows. My smack falls shy as he sashays out of reach. He flips his hair and shoots me a glare. He strolls through the bleachers. "Oh, relax! It's a joke. I'll get balanced first. Yeesh, no need to act like a big moral baby. Babies don't even learn right from wrong until they are, like, eight—so save the waterworks and find a different approach. Like a compass, point left for 'no, don't do that' and right for—" I reach down to pick up the knife I'd thrown earlier and it fumbles towards the ground. I reach to catch it and it slides through my grasp. The blade glides effortlessly through my skin. It clatters, spilling blood onto the brown sand. "Oh fuck. Ouch! Oh my God." A thin line on my palm slices opens as the fatty flesh separates. Blood seeps through the gash and pools down my wrist in a steady stream. I can't move. I'm frozen, staring at the source of fluid as my skin becomes hidden under a cloak of red. My mind swirls hazily as I scan for Calix. The room blurs, shifting as I stand straighter. I lose my breath. The pulsing in my ears is too loud. I wobble and sway, unsure which way is safe.

An arm wraps around my waist and steers me into the weapon room. Fingers work to wrap white fabric around the wound to apply pressure. Calix breathes an oath and I know my mom would never accept such profanity without delivering a bar of soap.

We stand in front of the stone tub, its murky contents still not cleaned out. Calix angles my swaddle down and I struggle to keep it up, remembering to elevate bleeding injuries. I know he may think it is good to clean a wound, but maybe dirty water wasn't the best idea.

"Belle, trust me. You're going to faint." I whirl to face him, but my vision blotches. Were the black spots his eyes or— He shoves my hand into the water. Its ice cold contents shock my skin and I gasp. My cut stings worse. The water seeps into the slice of skin like salt to an open wound. The cold contents burn my palm. I try to yank it out. Calix's grasp remains firm, holding the injury under the surface as I squirm. His broad shoulders flex, his arms stiffen, and I know it's a fight I'm destined to lose.

Then the pain weakens. My palm heats and tingles along the gash. The warmth dulls and the burn on my skin retreats to a tenderness. Calix releases my arm and pulls it out of the water. He unties the cloth and examines my palm. I peek at the damage. Where the laceration separated the skin a thin red line replaces it. The cut is closed and my palm is left a faint pink.

"How?" I whisper. I meant to sound stern, but losing blood will do that to you.

Calix shrugs, offering me a juice pouch I didn't see him grab. "Blue raspberry Kool-Aid? No flipping way!" I reach for it eagerly and stab at the plastic with the straw. I gulp until the bag wrinkles dry.

"The juice is to raise your blood sugar, but I didn't expect that reaction." Calix smirks. I punch him. My fist slaps against his naked skin. I glance down at his shirtless torso. His toned chest is smooth and hairless. Thin pink lines pattern across his skin. My eyes follow the indents of his biceps, his abdomen, to the drop by his waistline.

"Where the fuck is your shirt?" I blurt without any intention of looking up.

He points a perfect filed nail to the grey stone tub where a white cloth sits in a drenched heap. My swaddle.

"So, you saw a girl bleeding to death and thought: 'hey, let me take off my shirt and save her with my abs' before throwing my hand into the strange pit of unsanitary water?" I arch an eyebrow.

"Like what you see, huh?" His sarcastic smirk returns to its original place. My cheeks warm, but avoiding his stare means glimpsing the naked skin of his waistline.

He retrieves his shirt and pulls the wet fabric over his head. His messy black hair ruffles in different directions. He glides the wet material down his torso, a draping curtain that bunches with each tug before it's fully lowered. The show is over. There's no trace of blood on the white shirt as it sticks to his body and outlines his muscles. The thin, see-through fabric clings to his chest and flutters teasingly over his stomach. Was the shirt supposed to help?

"Blades are dipped in angel blood when they're forged. All our weapons are. And because Descendants have darkness in their veins the blade will harm you. Though, not as severely as a full-fledged demon. The blade is meant to extract darkness and defend the goodness of our angel heritage." He shrugs and his shirt lifts above his pant line. "They sting a little."

"A little." I scoff. "And that?" I jerk my chin at the tub.

He turns slowly, making a show of fearing the possible terror that lurks behind him. I narrow my eyes and win myself yet another one of his smirks.

"Oh, that. Obvious healing powers. Helps us keep training even if we're injured." He steps closer to me. I keep my stare on the ground and avoid the shape of his chest underneath the wet shirt.

"Belle," he murmurs.

I glimpse up from under his chin. He pulls a curl from my ponytail. His lips tug into a playful smile. His face lowers. I arch my neck and press myself against the wet fabric of his shirt. His hard stomach presses into my soft one and my cleavage squishes against his toned chest. His breath is cool against my warm cheeks.

A tremble shudders from the bulge on my thigh.

My phone vibrates in my pocket and I jump to check it. I pat my pants and pull out the small square. The excitement coursing through me as I think of the possibility of getting service and a text message. Is it Brett? Is she okay? I press a thumb against the touch screen and scan it for notifications.

A warning for low battery mocks me.

I put my phone away, back into its secure spot against my hip. I stare at the ground. The hope of leaving camp washes away like my earlier wound, but creates a fresh one. My throat tightens and my eyes prickle. I should not have felt so hopeful for contact. Stupid me. And yet, a part of me wonders why I can't communicate between camps. If I could just contact someone to discover where she's situated. *Camp is meant to teach you balance and sometimes you realize what makes you lack it, are the certain ties you carry. They will not place you based on familiarity.* I know it's true.

I stare at the grey stone floor, examining how the rocks have dented and smoothed over with time. The fluorescent light casts a shadow on my shoes. It sways, away then closer. Calix grunts. My cheeks heat at the thought of what almost happened. I peek up from my lashes at Calix. He's motionless, staring at something next to us. I relax and exhale, standing straighter.

"You won't reach your boyfriend here, I'm afraid." His eyes are black and his face composed in a mask of emotionless fury.

He clenches his jaw and pinches his brows together. I step back. Opening and closing my mouth, I don't know what to say. I reach for him to close the distance, but he pulls away. He rolls his eyes, as if reading my thoughts of desperation and confirms that his feelings are all in my imagination. He doesn't want me. He could have anyone. Why would he care how the situation ended when he can start it up with someone else? He walks through the arched doorway and into the bleachers. I follow, rushing to keep up.

I want to scream. It's not what he thinks. I wanted to hear from Brett. He's so annoying. I wasn't thinking of Jeremy. Stunned at the last thought, I snap my mouth shut. Maybe I should have thought of him. I forgot about my boyfriend and one glance at Calix tells me he already forgot about me. His back is stiff and he doesn't look my way. I trip over the stairs. If what almost happened was nothing then I will treat it as that.

"Breakfast is soon. We will take the Doctrine tunnel and steer towards Residence," he commands, his tone so formal no one would believe I made him laugh five minutes ago. I follow the route I planned earlier. Another thing I will not let him know, pride isn't something to commend.

I trail behind him. Moonlight trickles through the skylights overhead and peeps through archways of the Doctrine tunnel. I glance into the Meeting Square. A breakfast table floats from the pile on the dead grass and places itself in the sand turf. The table underneath is quick to follow. I pause and Calix stops to check on me, probably concerned about another bleeding episode. He follows my gaze and nods.

"Hurry, before Zilla notices us. We have a few hours before we are scheduled to wake up." He strolls through the tunnel. His posture nonchalant as another table floats across the Square.

"Enchanted tables that come out at meal time by themselves?" Moving the tables and chairs to the dead grass and back every time we eat is too much unnecessary effort.

Calix turns with his eyebrows raised and a look that questions my sanity. He glances to the Square and then to me. Finally showing concern for what I see.

I point at a floating table as it unstacks and settles into the next row. It hovers and drops against the sand with a thud. Right in front of Zilla. Her arm stretches out in front of her and her fingertips follow the motion of the next table as it lifts from the side of the Square and places itself in the sand.

"What the fuck?"

Calix grabs my arm and pulls me away. "Isabelle, we don't have time for this." He grunts against my weight and I plant my feet into the ground, refusing to move without any answers.

"Zilla has magic powers?" He huffs and then whips around. In a quick motion his shoulder finds my stomach and I'm lifted up. My head bobs against his back. I wiggle and bang my fists on his butt. His wet shirt is cold against the night air and smells like wet laundry.

"Let me down you insanely strong idiot!"

"Shut up!" he hisses. He throws me on my feet. "Do you hear yourself? You are situated at a camp where affinities are what Descendants train to acquire one day. Some people do not share their powers without a Summoning. And yes, our lead Preceptor has a useful skill, but you cannot stop and gawk while we are trying to avoid being caught out past curfew. So can you start walking, please?" I nod, and spin, flipping my ponytail before I go.

Calix sighs and follows.

We swish through the door of Residence and Peter swivels on his chair. His bald head reflects the light from the lamp on the front desk. Out of the four Preceptors, Peter is the most quiet and uninteresting. He nods along and wears his matching coat. Power does not ripple off him like Zilla, or glint hungrily in his eyes like Caradoc, or weigh on his shoulders like Julius.

"We couldn't sleep so we went to Ordnance to train," Calix says. Man, am I happy to have him next to me now. If you are going to get in trouble, having a *commendable* partner in crime is helpful.

Peter stares, taking a moment to process what Calix said. He glances between Calix's wet shirt and my soaked cleavage. My cheeks burn. Peter nods and rolls his chair to the desk.

Chapter 16

I trudge my feet through the sand of the Meeting Square. I rub my eyes and stifle a yawn. At least I'm awake and on time. Onyx struts beside me, wearing her electric-blue stilettos and a shirt cropped above her midriff. Her leather jacket hangs to her waist, reinstating to onlookers that she is, in fact, a badass. She flips her red hair and it whips me in the eye. I grunt. An hour of sleep will deprive you of the ability to form sentences.

"Hey, Isabelle, ready for Force? Or should I say ready for, *papacito rico*?" Lara shimmies on her side of the bench.

"He's sooo hot!" Rachel, her brain sister, pipes in and licks her lips.

I shuffle forward. I don't understand Spanish. I wear my best "hell yeah" face, which, with an hour of sleep, I'm pretty sure comes across as a full body cringe. If Lara takes offence to my lack of enthusiasm she doesn't show it, beckoning us to the table with an empty plate.

Rachel leans the other way to talk to a boy with chubby cheeks and metallic-blue eyes. Ash calls him Brody, demanding his attention from across the table with a half-lidded glare and dropped chin. Brody holds up his palm and flips non-existent long hair. He brushes invisible air under his cropped brown buzz cut and stretched lobe ears. Ash doesn't glance up as we approach, too determined to glare at Brody. He impatiently thrums his fingers against the table, hoping to annoy his friend into answering. "If looks could kill" isn't a cliché when you attend a camp full of angel Descendants searching for a spiritual affinity. And yet, Ash still manages to have the illegitimate talent.

I examine the crowd of breakfast goers and glimpse the brown grass in the corner of the Square. "Onyx, when someone has an affinity, why isn't it used in the open?"

Onyx sighs, but doesn't stop. She sashays around the table and plops herself in front of Lara. She pats the spot next to her with her black-polished nails. "Sometimes we get caught up in hiding it from the naked eye. Those without Sight are vulnerable and witnessing affinities may cause instability for those who are weaker. Most of the time the Blind justify it as something else, but you never know who's watching." She shrugs.

"But how come at camp, we're not more open?" I slide in and grab a pancake.

Onyx reaches for bacon with her fingers and takes a bite. Her dark red lipstick glistens with grease. "I guess it's more so no one is discouraged or singled out. Everyone finds their own way and how they want to use their affinity. Then again, some affinities may be as common as never missing a target, strength, or in the way people listen to you. Could even be in tech support or changing a lightbulb." If my affinity is changing a dead bulb I will be so bummed out. I want something cool like elasticity. Then again, all those years of ballet class and performing in the back killed *that* possibility.

Cattia walks to the table with a glass of orange juice. She turns her body towards Lara, veiling herself from view with unnatural, straightened blonde hair. "Hey, that's my seat," she places a small fist on her hip and frowns at Lara.

"*Quien fue a Sevilla, perdió su silla.* If you leave your place, you lose it." Lara flips her black hair and continues to shove diced watermelon slices into her mouth.

"Yup, he who went to Seville lost his chair," Rachel translates. Cattia grinds her teeth and Lara forks more fruit onto her plate. Onyx wipes her fingers on a napkin and reaches for a piece of ham, taking a bite of it slowly, never missing a movement from Cattia.

"I would like it if you moved." Cattia places her drink down with a thud. Onyx nudges me and I don't have to look her way to know that she's rubbing her palms together.

"Yeah, I'll move when I'm done." Lara waves her fork at her and continues to eat, oblivious to Cattia's strained face and scrunched fists.

I peek at Onyx. Her lips purse, eyes bulge, and when Cattia flips her streaked blonde hair Onyx erupts in fits of laughter. She points a sharp nail at Lara and Cattia as if trying to fill in the blanks. They ignore her.

"Oh and, Isabelle, you should sleep in your own bed at night or the bags under your eyes won't be the only ones you find at breakfast." Cattia says. I sit, mouth open, staring at her staticky hair as she twirls away. Onyx's laughter drops to silence as she gasps for air.

Cattia struts to the next table and squeezes into the seat next to Calix. He stares as she waves at me. A smirk on his lips and eyebrows raised under his tousled bangs. I look away, untucking my hair from behind my ear. It hangs in a curled curtain, hiding myself from the neighbouring breakfast bench.

"What the fuck?" I search the table for an explanation, hoping it is written on someone else's face. Ash, Brody, Rachel and Lara stare at their plates.

"Girl, you were out again last night?" Onyx laughs and wiggles her red eyebrows. "You got a little wild side, don't you?" I groan and drop my head on the table. The wood ridges press into my forehead. I roll to peek up at her. She ruffles my hair. "Don't worry. She's a jealous bitch, we already know she has a crush on Calix. Who, by the way, keeps looking over here, most likely wondering if we're talking about him like the egotistical snob he is." Onyx holds up the middle finger. I reach to push it down. "I'm surprised she can sit with that stick so far up her ass."

"*Moro viejo nunca será buen cristiano.*" Lara shrugs, reaching for some grapes.

"Okay, where's the remote, I must have changed the language settings." Onyx pretends to search under her plate and under the table.

"I said the old Moor will never be a good Christian." Lara narrows her eyes.

"You can't change someone." Rachel agrees.

"And with that outburst, I think Cattia has lived away from Seattle too long," Lara says. Rachel nods beside her brain sister.

"How long has she lived at camp?" Onyx asks.

"Two years, arrived before me and Rachel." The two girls bob their heads in synchronization.

They continue to talk about time at the camp, who's been here longest, who's recruited, and who grew up on a reserve. Normally, I'd take interest and ask how long the average person trains at camp, but Cattia flips her straightened hair and squeezes Calix's bicep.

He squints down at her through his dark lashes. His smirk is gone. I wonder what she says when she tilts back and laughs. Calix listens, no amusement on his face, but no boredom, either. Her hand doesn't move from his arm, unless you count the pats she places when she tells another punchline. Last night, the wet shirt outlined his body into vivid rivets of muscle. The definition in his biceps and stomach were exposed under the fabric. My cheeks feel hot and I turn to my pancakes. I glance down at the newly etched red line on my hand. The skin is no longer tender. I close my fist and play with the edges of my napkin.

"Wait. She's Caradoc's daughter? No way!" Onyx places a piece of bacon down on her plate, using the dish for the first time this morning.

"Who?" I ask, looking between Onyx and Lara. They huddle closer over plates of dismissed watermelon.

"Did you check out again? For real, stay in tonight and sleep. And eat more meat—your boobs are looking smaller."

Onyx places some ham and bacon onto my plate along with a fresh stack of pancakes.

"Mary-Anne," Lara says, answering my question and stabbing some meat with her fork.

"She's Caradoc's daughter?" They nod. No wonder the poor girl always looks so scared; Caradoc is an intimidating Preceptor. Not as scary as Zilla, but close.

"She's moved between camps her whole life, I heard. Caradoc has worked as a Preceptor at multiple locations before he settled here or that's how the story goes. Don't ask me how long he's situated here though, I don't know. It's not like you can ask them—it's weird. But Calix has lived here the longest, he probably remembers the shifts of Preceptors and Descendants." I try not to react to the mention of his name, but my pulse quickens. I sit straighter, avoiding the blonde movement at the next table.

The Preceptors gain power from the Blind, leading us into balance, reforming us into working warriors with affinities. They act as professors in a private education. Isn't that why we prepare for the Summoning? We're called to duty based on what we can offer as a Descendant. Our affinities utilized to defend those who are ignorant or without angel lineage. My blood will excel at something I have no control over and provide me with a destined role. There goes the dream of veterinary school.

I glance around the Square, watching other Descendants, waiting for them to perform something unordinary, a peek at an affinity. I search for Zilla, confirming her power last night left me needing more proof. Julius and Peter are situated at opposite corners of the breakfast area. Caradoc and Zilla absent. Julius catches my eye and waves. His ponytail sways as he glances from me to Onyx, shaking his head as if knowing we're causing trouble. He bounces on the balls of his feet, unable to abandon his post but his eyes twinkle with the desire to join in on the fun.

Onyx is on her feet before I can get a glimpse of her expression. Her stiletto shoes puncture the sand as she marches her way across the clearing. I peel my thighs off the wooden bench and join her to say hi. Julius' boyish grin grows bigger. Onyx stands with her arms crossed along her torso, propping up her small boobs. She looms over him, his two inch advantage gone, and gulps up all his personal space with a menacing sneer. I misread the situation. I glance at my half eaten pancakes, a longing wish to sit in an area of cease fire.

"Stop tormenting my friends," she snarls. I wiggle myself in between Onyx and Julius. They don't break eye contact. My short legs peg me in the middle of a conversation that I am not part of.

"Hello, guys. Switzerland!" I sing.

"So, I can't say hi to other people at camp because they may know you? That's ridiculous!" His hands fling in the air. They're a thin bony finger away from whacking me in the nose.

"Glad we have an understanding. Don't talk, ever. You're more attractive that way." Onyx whips around, launching herself back in the direction of the table. She kisses Ash on the cheek before she leaves. Julius swears under his breath and retreats into Residence, abandoning his post. I'm stuck in one spot, rotating my focus between both my friends.

Plates clatter and cutlery clinks as people start to jostle. A few stragglers start the motion, until only breakfast latecomers are left sitting at the wooden table benches shoveling cold eggs into their already full mouths. Bodies move in the direction of the tunnels of Doctrine, others charge towards the walkway of Ordnance. I shrug my way to the centre archway. The familiar shade of Doctrine casts a cool breeze around me. My hair sticks to the sweat on my neck. I cut left towards the stairway.

I shift my feet, moving with the flow of bodies. Farther down the hall, a head of fair hair bobs. I push myself forward, propelling through a wall of limbs and muttering few apologies. My feet edge against the uneven stone floor, unsure of my awkward footing as I tiptoe to maintain my view of her. A few more shoves and some swear words and I'm free.

"Hey, Mary-Anne." I fall into step next to her. My shoulder brushes hers with each stride.

"Oh, hey..." She doesn't look at me. Her thin frame swims under an oversized T-shirt and her brown eyes sink into her face. Her shoulder blades poke through the thin cotton. Her pale skin cracks where orange foundation overlaps a poorly covered zit. She's taller than I am. Around the same weight, except where I have curves her willowy body remains levelled flat. She's closer to Brett's age than mine.

"I'm Isabelle. We have Sound together. Ash's friend." She nods. Our feet clomp up the steps of the stairway. Okay, maybe I'm not good at this. "I know he is sometimes intimidating, but he means well. He's not tutoring you in *big and tough* is he?" She doesn't laugh. I mentally summon for her to spill why she's really seeing Ash. If something is unravelling between Onyx and Ash I have to help. The two aren't as close as when they sat on the train. They wouldn't tell me if anything happened. Onyx isn't one to vent and I'm not one to pry. Well, not the direct first-party kind of pry.

Mary-Anne sighs, reluctant to share any answers with me. I wait. Patience in exchange for her trust. "He's okay. I just feel bad. He tries hard to help me."

"Oh, I'm sure you'll get it. Keep trying and you are bound to improve. Anything fun I can try on my own?" Hopefully he's helping her with private lessons not having *private* lessons. I don't want those kinds of tips.

"I wish. I can't even find a melody when I listen to jazz. My dad, he's pushing me, you know?" How can Ash help another Descendant when he's recently recruited? Mary-Anne has lived here for years. I can't imagine enrolling in low-balance Sound for that long.

Mary-Anne pauses, mistaking my silence for lack of interest. "Sorry, didn't mean to spill that on you. Anyway, I'm in this hall." She points towards the second tunnel from the stairway, more advanced in Sight than I am, but not enough to excel. "Tell Ash

I appreciate what he's doing. I know he thinks his affinity isn't much, but it's helping." Her dry lips crack as she smiles.

I nod, unable to say more. Ash has an affinity for Sound? Who else has discovered their excelled Sense. Was there a general list of all possible affinities like a diagnosis? The only one I can imagine for Sound is superhearing, if that is a thing. Sound of Truth… Ash barely even says anything aside from his share of unwanted opinions and few grunts. How can someone hide a part of them so well?

I tromp to the middle hallway of Sight and take my spot next to the girl with rusty red hair. Razielle. A pit in my stomach forms as I think of Onyx. It doesn't matter. Or that's what I tell myself. I arrived here without luggage and I expect to have friends. That's not how the world works. A week ago I had a sister to take care of and Jeremy as help. As days pass I realize I never had control over, either. Brett is independent. Caring for her is an excuse that made me feel part of a family still. Jeremy fell into pattern with my life, never a separate entity, but always there. Bonds aren't forged in a week.

Everyone finds their own way and how they want to use their affinity. Right, it is Ash's choice who he tells. I groan and sink deeper into my desk. I can't help but feel excluded.

I remember my mouth moving and the flow of voices as discussions echo from stone rooms, but the content never sticks.

I shuffle towards Residence, determined to find answers. Descendants pass me in the halls all faceless except for one.

Calix approaches in dark jeans and a snug black t-shirt. His gaze focuses on me. Something flashes in his eyes, but before I can read the expression the emotion melts into the dark brown and hides behind his usual cocky smirk. "Belle." He nods.

"Not now, Calix." I brush past him.

His fingers find my wrist. Warm skin laces against mine as he restrains me from stepping another foot farther. I yank my arm, but my strength isn't in it. His touch soothes my need to break free and blurs my thoughts. His grip doesn't budge, keeping me in place and holding my shoulder against his.

"About last night," he whispers.

"It's fine," I interject. Unlike Jeremy, Calix doesn't buy it. Where Jeremy would give me space before another attempt at fixing a problem, Calix won't release my arm until it means forgiveness.

He stares at me, and the earlier glimmer returns in his eyes. The blackness fades, melting into the colour of liquid caramel. His pupils widen, his eyebrows lower, and his cheeks slump, releasing his usual tension. Light freckles line the bridge of his nose like constellations.

"I don't like Cattia." He frees his grip, tucking his fists into his pockets. His footsteps are silent as he leaves me, frozen and alone.

Chapter 17

Ash's room is located on the same floor as mine. I hike up the steps, holding my breath to cover my erratic breathing. If Onyx is with him then I'll receive answers from them together. They both skipped out on dinner and I had another gut-wrenching moment of exclusion.

I sat at the table expecting Onyx to join so I could ask her about Ash and his affinity. Neither of them came. Instead, I hunched over split peas and poked at glazed chicken as Cattia ignored my existence and Lara gushed over Oliver, our instructor. Calix didn't show up, either. Not that I cared.

I left the table on a mission. I sprint through the hall and stumble as a door slams up ahead. Slowing my pace, I squint into the shadows. The air ruffles fabric with a sound like a plastic tarp in the wind. Shoes click closer. The silhouette grows taller as the distance closes. When the light doesn't reflect off red hair I flatten against the wall.

His silver hair bounces against the collar of his chestnut cloak. Bronze-framed glasses rest on the hook of his nose and his grey eyes peer over, boring into mine. His paper-thin lips pinch up and it's not in welcome.

"Isabelle. Shouldn't you take part in dinner?" Caradoc sneers. His accent sings each word in a cruel sonnet.

"I'm looking for my friends," I say, my back straightening.

"Yes, the Measure and the Warrior... How unfortunate of a situation." He drops his chin, waiting for an objection. I smack my lips together. "I see even Calix has warmed to you. He is one of the best. Someone it would be a shame to lose."

When I don't respond, his lips curl up into a sadistic smile. His wild grey eyes brighten against his porcelain skin, adding colour to his complexion. His slender cheeks stretch against his face bones, so feeble they may tear. He angles his lean shoulders over me as he leers down. My back presses against the cool stone wall.

"Third door on the right," he says.

His cold breath blows across my face. I hold mine. Caradoc strides away. His leather overcoat flaps against his ankles. Flecks of light glint off his silver hair as he disappears into the shadows.

I scurry down the hall. One. Two. Three. I feel for the cool knob and stumble into a black walled room.

"Guys, Caradoc said some weird shit— Oh!" Colour rushes to my face and my gaze drops to my runners. Unsure if I should close the door and leave or if it's too late, I stand there, stuck.

Brody pulls his arms away from Ash's neck and scoots to the other end of the bed. Ash untangles his legs and runs his fingers through his unusually messy hair. Brody wipes his lips with a thumb. Ash glowers.

"Okay, bitches, I have the snacks." Onyx stumbles into the room carrying cylinder chips, Skittles and a bag of liquorice. She staggers and her eyebrows almost touch when she realizes who she bumps. "Isabelle?"

My gaze darts between Ash, the boy he kissed and his girlfriend.

"I should have knocked." I try to pull the door closed in front of me.

"Yes. You should have, sweetheart." Ash says, his voice cool.

"We skipped dinner for a movie night. It's Friday." Onyx weighs each word, listening for a problem like someone of guilt would search for a hole in their alibi. "You could join if you want, no need to lose a boob over it. I guess leaving you with Cattia wasn't cool."

"Onyx," Ash says. "She knows."

"What?" Onyx whirls around. Her black eyes grow darker.

"I should have knocked." I repeat.

"You have a lot to talk about." Brody frowns. "I'll excuse myself." He rises from the mattress wearing skinny jeans and a cable-knit sweater. The holes in his ears from spacer earrings are as big as a toonie coin. Ash remains seated, watching as Brody shuts the door.

"So…" I toe the edge of the carpet.

"I'm gay," Ash says.

"And Brody is?" I ask, sneaking a look at Onyx.

"My roommate," Ash nods.

"But I thought you two were—" Onyx told me they were together. She refused Julius' advances. Kissed Ash… on the cheek. They never displayed much affection, only respect and familiarity. Onyx did get cozy with him on the train after I asked if he was gay.

"Let us explain." Onyx gestures towards the rolling chair by the desk. I sit, swiveling to keep them both in view. "We come from a reserve. We grew up with strict stories from the Bible, trained so we can eventually defend the good in our blood. With strict beliefs, well, Adam and Eve, not Adam and Steve." She shrugs. "Our parents are good friends so we're practically married off, but that doesn't change the truth. We grew up, our feelings changed. I love Ash, but we love differently. Our community isn't ready to accept gays, so as long as this story remains feasible Ash is protected."

"It's a debt I can never repay." Ash stares at Onyx as she speaks. His eyes glimmer with a respect I never noticed.

"I'm sorry you have to hide." I move to sit on the bed next to him. "Maybe if you try to tell them… Oh God, I sound cliché don't I? I won't tell anyone." He nods. Onyx exhales.

"And I'll start locking the door." He groans.

"It's my fault, I said I'd come right back and then I ran into… It doesn't matter. We'll act more carefully." Onyx plumps onto the mattress, passing me the bag of Skittles.

"How do you even know which room is mine?" Ash asks.

"Caradoc told me. He was in the hall. Do Preceptors have rooms in the Residence?" Now it's my turn to ask the questions.

"I think they're situated on the main floor somewhere, easy access to the Meeting Square. Weird that he was upstairs, probably doing a security check." She shrugs. I don't mention that he came out of a room. He could have done a round through Residence to check to make sure no one wandered into a vacant dorm.

"He said something about the Measure and the Warrior. What does that mean?" They look at each other, silently communicating if they should tell me the truth. "Look, if it has to do with Ash having an affinity I know that, too." Let me help them speed along the process.

"Wow. I underestimated you. Must be the big-tits stereotype. You are smart. I knew I liked you for a reason." Onyx exposes her pearl teeth under her black glossed lips.

"I have an affinity in Sound. I excel in understanding tempo difference and change. I have achieved average balance, which is why I do not attend classes. I am a Measure," Ash murmurs, his voice never changing in tone.

"If you have an affinity and you're balanced, why weren't you Summoned? Did you come here to tutor?" They exchange another look.

"I came here to remain with Onyx. A tutoring position is a favour from Zilla, which I find myself enjoying. My affinity is not exactly an advantage or in demand," Ash says, picking his words carefully.

"So when you're not Summoned to work, what happens?" I ask, hoping the answer isn't a life stuck in secrecy within a local camp.

"You live how you want. You can always reject the offer made, but mostly they are too enticing to pass up. You'll always have a choice, sweetheart," Ash says.

"And you, do you have an affinity?" About to deny it, I cut her off. "A warrior?"

"When you live on a reserve you know your lineage to understand what traits your ancestors had and will pass on to you. My father and mother are both guards and defenders, they are called in during times of crises. I am expected to have the same affinity in Force. I was sent here to train."

"Can definitely see you kicking a few asses." And so we have it. The truth.

"Just a few?" Onyx looks hurt. "Take that back and I won't make you the reason for my christening." She reaches around Ash and thuds her first into my shoulder. I rub the tender spot. She laughs and Ash joins in. I open the Skittles, but Onyx steals the bag. Ash reaches for the remote and flicks on the small screen.

"Hey, how'd you get a TV in your room?" I ask.

"Onyx's credit card."

Chapter 18

The weeks blur the longer I stay here. My schedule becomes a routine not numbered by the days, but by the training exercises I complete. The thing about Sight of Knowing and Sound of Truth is that they go together. If someone told you everything at once, you wouldn't believe it. In time you learn to ask the right questions and find honesty in what you hear.

I still worry about Brett and Jeremy, but I accept that I cannot help them while I'm here. I practice every night, occasionally alone, but Calix is somewhat helpful. I'd never tell him that though. He's still annoying as ever with his mysterious past and his inability to say exactly what he's thinking. I will get out eventually and reunite with my sister, but I know I have to stay here for now. Leaving too early would result in exposure to darkness. I intend to conquer it.

Rejections have occurred more frequently the past couple of days. The first took place with Jonathan, then a girl named Eileen, then Jessica. Now it's a young boy Tim. His blue eyes stare at me as red liquid streaks his face. Blood. It oozes from his nose and between his lips. His blond hair sticks to his forehead as he convulses in the centre of the circle. My arms link with Onyx's and Lara's. Some students use their affinities to bind him from escaping, but that's why we hold together. Now comes the final prayer as the Preceptors chant and someone aims. Then comes an executioner Summoned for the camp. What a shitty duty. The eyes of the young boy widen. An arrow pierces his skull. A clean shot in the middle of light eyebrows.

Calix pulls me away and sits me on the wooden lunch bench. He wipes at my face with a cool cloth and rubs my arms. The friction is meant to warm up my body, but it's the middle of summer and I'm sweating. My perspiration is cold against my skin and I'm shaking. Like wearing a snowsuit and feeling hot in negative-degree weather.

Tim's eyes, so much like my sister's. And Calix knows that. He's listened to my anecdotes and imagined plans for the future once I get out. He stopped trying to fight me on leaving and found it is better to play along. Although I know I'll go, he's set on having me here.

"Belle." He sighs. A cool breath of spearmint lands on my face. "It won't be her. Ever."

"How do you know?" I look into his brown eyes and he doesn't move. He stares, rooted in one spot, not running.

"Because she is a part of you," he says, so sure of himself that I believe him.

"Thank you." I play with the hem of my sleeve, twisting and untwisting the bunched fabric. He tugs a curl.

"Let's go shoot."

My knife pierces the waxwork dummy in the shoulder and sticks. An arrow punctures the heart.

"Show off." I mutter. I reach for the blade. The tip is lodged in the material and I wiggle it free. The knife leaves a punctured slit in the plastic.

"Your shot is good." Calix smirks.

"But yours is better?" I ask.

"Yup." He wraps an arm around my shoulder and shakes me. His chest rumbles with laughter. I nudge myself under his armpit and my arm crams against his sack of arrows. He smells like sweat and laundry.

His muscles tense and his body turns rigid. I expect what will happen next. When he takes a step away from me I understand it's because he caught himself getting too close. The physical distance an excuse for the mental. I don't respond, just nod. Another routine I have grown used to.

We shoot a couple more rounds. My throws continue to leave spikes of knives in the dummy. Calix demonstrates a clean shot every time. To stick the blade and achieve perfect aim seems impossible. My strike is either a few inches from my initial target or punctured at an angle. I can never perfect both. I rehearse spin throws and axe tosses until I'm sore.

My shoulder bumps with Calix's as we hike up the bleachers. Someone snickers from the top step. A head of blond curls bounces past us to the centre of the arena. Cattia whispers into Rachel's ear and the girls both chuckle too loud to sound natural. Rachel flips her black hair, exposing a bottom layer of blond. I saunter away, not bothering to find out what weapon she picks or if she has a good shot, no matter how curious I am. I don't dare. I stopped caring when she tried to kiss Calix at the dinner table, spoiling the taste of my chicken pot pie. So much for a nice Southern roommate.

"Belle." He stops and I know he's going to try and make up for the attack that happened earlier to distract me from their presence. But I don't want to talk about Brett, or Cattia and her perfect ringlets. I care about my sister and leaving. Calix isn't mine, but Brett is.

"It's fine," I say.

He pauses, gripping my arm to stop me. The dark staircase conceals us from the giggling girls in the arena. Their laughter dances up towards us. A sinister reminder that I can't leave. It's not like school where you get to go home. This is my home and the heckler is my roommate. I sigh, there are worst things. I imagine Tim's blue eyes, fearful and young, staring up at the faces that form the circle around him, not strong enough to fight off the parasite of darkness. I cringe.

Calix can't see me, but he feels the twitch through his grip. "You're not fine." He searches for me in the shadows. His fingers find my hair in the dark. He plays with a stray curl along my collarbone. His fingertips trail heated lines against my neck.

Calix has lived at the camp since he was thirteen. No one knows how he arrived, only that he did. He's balanced, some say he came that way, which is rare for someone so young. Now he's twenty-three, but an affinity hasn't surfaced, which is also rare for someone already balanced. To summarize, he's a freak. Okay, maybe he's just different and has a hard time admitting it.

I place a hand on his, holding it still.

"Let's go eat." And we do.

Chapter 19

Descendants line the stone bleachers and hunch together in hushed whispers. A murmur runs through the gym like a soft hum. Calix sits in the front row. His black hair shakes, causing the long strands to take their natural messy place. Onyx pulls my arm to lead me to the top. A trouble maker who sits at the back of the class. Lara flanks her other side and Brody and Ash lean together against the wall, touching arms and nothing else. Rachel and Cattia sit on the other side of the dome, their blonde hair like a beacon signaling disaster.

If Lara is annoyed by her brain sister's new-found bestie, she doesn't show it. Her green eyes watch Oliver prowl the bleachers for a spot. She waves at him with her fingers.

"Hey, Oliver! *Tienes novia?*" She whistles. Onyx snorts

Oliver squeezes himself through the legs of the people in front of us, shoving to get closer to where we sit. "Hello." He greets us warmly. She winks at him from under a straight line of bangs. He rolls up the sleeves of his dress shirt, exposing ink lines on his forearm. Tattoos of script and roses blemish his bulging veins as he grips a leather-bound journal. Lara fans herself and pretends to fall on our laps. We giggle.

"*Dejame estar contigo,*" Lara whines, holding her fists to her chest, pretending to clench her heart. "*Quiero hacerte el amor.*" She drops her fists to her hips and swivels her thighs in a seductive thrust. I snort and Onyx covers her mouth to conceal her laughter.

Zilla calls Oliver to the centre of the gym to join Aliza and other familiar instructors. Before he leaves, he turns around. Lara drops her fists in her lap and sits straight. She's the poster child for a perfect student. Onyx's face is as red as her hair as she works to contain another spurt of laughter.

Oliver smiles. He strokes Lara's bangs, brushing them away for a better view of her green eyes. "*Tienes los ojos más bonitos del mundo. Te deseo.*" He bows with an arm extended forward then drifts into the crowd to claim his post.

My mouth pops and I'm sure it's hanging open. Lara's jaw drops, her mouth clamps shut and her eyes widen.

"What did he just say?" I ask.

"He said I have the prettiest eyes in the world." Lara gulps. "*Te deseo*. I desire you."

Onyx holds a fist out for her to bump it, but Lara doesn't see as she stares after Oliver.

"And you thought he didn't notice you. Well, looky here. Turns out he's the only one that understands half the shit you're saying." Onyx snorts. Ash leans forward to place a hand on Lara's shoulder to offer her his social-condolences.

"Descendants," Zilla's voice booms through the bleachers, echoing off the walls. The chatter stops and the dome falls silent.

"To those of you who are recruited you may have heard talk of our year-end Summoning. For those of you who have not, it is a ritual where we select Descendants for their abilities in the four Senses and their remarkable balance. Each lesson and exercise teaches you to maintain balance in your spirit and goodness, and strengthens your performance. Those who have achieved a steady pace and were awarded their affinity, we will welcome you into a new position of honour. It is a moment of recognition that we, as Preceptors, do not take lightly. The significance will define you in our community and open up opportunity in your future. We hope all Descendants here will inherit their destined birthright of power and potential."

Caradoc steps forward. "With great delight, we announce that the approaching Summoning is scheduled to take place here at our camp. Recruited students from all regional locations will travel here to celebrate our annual event. We will welcome them with the utmost respect. As I know will you."

Peter raises his arms. "Today, as a form of training and preparation we will demonstrate the importance of affinities and provide a lesson for each Sense. As Preceptors we excel in each and encourage you to join us."

Julius' smile is bright, even from the back row. Onyx chews the skin around her fingernails. "Due to the recent attacks we will push the Summoning up, in need of recruited bodies to help defend the balance of mankind. Everyone is a Descendant, not only the ones who attend camp. As a region we have decided it is best to situate more people in everyday life and Exorcise those who are weak and in need of help. Summonings will now take place at each core solstice, twice a year. The transition of summer and winter will guide our change in the balance of Sight, Sound, Voice, and Force. We believe with our direct teachings, we will help you all reach your potential. We are here for you."

Zilla announces, "Welcome to Doctrine Day."

Descendants separate into groups and instructors rotate to test our balance in each Sense. The Preceptors monitor, offering their help and demonstration of power. There is no way of knowing how to teach Descendants specific affinities because blood excels in Senses differently. The recruited have no awareness of their linage so it is hard to train while waiting for signs of strength. By examining reactions and efforts in simple tests Descendants are able to graduate levels and practice harder exercises. If someone is further along in one Sense compared to the others, it becomes obvious where they are destined. For those who come from a reserve, their lineage plays a role in their placement. An Exorcist sent me to the camp for Sight because I displayed weakness in the Sense, this is why we meditate after lessons—to feel the truth in what we learn.

"Force comes from your mind, your physical capability, and your spirit." Zilla leads a discussion on the Touch of Force. Students huddle around the ends of her oil-coloured cloak. I sit cross-legged on the floor next to Brody. He leans his body forward, absorbing everything she says. Onyx, Lara, and I were separated into different groups. There's no way it was a fluke. Part of the disadvantages of familiarity.

Brody and I haven't talked much since I found out Ash lived with his boyfriend and Onyx is a cover. The relationship became an accepted topic, like coming to camp meant I had to swallow a lot of things that I didn't believe were possible before. That is, Ash having a soft side. A month ago I'd scold Brett about stories similar to the ones I'm living and convince her it's not real. Now, I wish I could hug her for all the doubt I placed in her imagination. If I could descend from a fallen angel, inherit spiritual essence that may lead to discovering an affinity or rejection of life, then Brody should know I'm comfortable with his relationship with Ash.

"As some may know, I am a Transport. My affinity is often referred to as telekinesis." An arrow floats out of Calix's sack and thrusts into the waxwork dummy. The fletching twirls and blurs, blue and red blending into purple. The speed plummets the point into the foam chest, burrowing deeper before breaking the shaft. The arrow head lodges into the skin of its victim. Zilla stands, palms clasped. "I can transport items where I want, though it takes great effort to practice how I want the object to arrive." She motions an introduction to the instructor of Touch. Oliver slumps in the spotlight casually. His thick-framed glasses, wide chest and brown cowlick make him look like a tattooed Clark Kent. "Some have variations of this affinity."

Oliver strides into the clearing and holds out an empty palm. The broken shaft of the arrow appears in his grasp. "I can manipulate the location of an item, but I can't move it. I also can't teleport myself, which is always everyone's favourite question." He smiles a dimpled grin that would leave Lara paralyzed and me with a puddle of drool to mop.

"These affinities are considered Touch because we operate objects through the force of our mind's wish, rather than a physical touch applying force. Our affinities are an example to how Touch of Force is a mirrored Sense, just as all four are. A Descendant can excel in Touch through physical strength and offer active affinities, or the Force of a power unseen. There are no limitations," Zilla concludes. Hands shoot up, distorting my view as a blur of silver hair approaches. Some Descendants ask if Zilla knew of her lineage, if she's been in battle and how much concentration she uses to move things. All the burning questions that have circled around camp and curious rumours, receive their answers. Zilla entered battle once, but left after losing a dear friend. Specifics weren't given. She came to camp as a recruit and it took a vast amount of exercises and a few incidents to figure out what her mind wanted to do. Her answer included an anecdote of throwing a vase at her first boyfriend in frustration without intending to. Now her affinity works like stretching a muscle, requiring little concentration. Brett would love that.

Caradoc steps forward, cutting off any further questions and demanding we focus on the use of the darkness as well as the good to achieve full balance. In only focusing on the good like most Preceptors teach—he shoots a glare towards Zilla—we diminish a part of our heritage.

"Balance is achieved with good and bad, lightness and darkness. Your focus on the angel will not change the dilution of your blood. Balance in Sight, Voice, Sound and Touch require the stability of understanding yourself and your inheritance. As Preceptors we teach you ignorance has resulted in the construction of camps, the death of warriors, the exorcism of the weak. So why lack consciousness of the blood that dilutes the angel? Remember your ancestor, but don't forget the lineage that divides you." Caradoc's voice booms from between sealed lips, or at least it didn't look like they moved. His face is grave, eyes wildly moving over the crowd around him.

"My affinity is in Voice. It is an example of Voice of Reason as a shared entity. The ability to public speak and woo a crowd." He nods before exiting the base of the dome. We are left, huddling together and trying to decipher if his earlier speech is an example of convincing us something untrue or a persuasion of the truth.

Peter, the quiet Preceptor, walks towards our group as Zilla rotates over to the next one. Peter's brows are knit, staring after Caradoc's silver hair.

"Hello." He clears his throat. Unsure where to look he rests his stare above our heads towards the exit tunnel. "I, well. I'm Peter, I excel in Sound." He looks over his shoulder. His voice never changing in tone as he fumbles over his sentence.

Aliza, my instructor in Sound, skips forward and waves at the group. "He is the epitome of Sound of Truth because he can always tell when you lie." She gestures towards Peter. He lowers his gaze and his bald head starts to perspire. "Not exactly a great affinity to have on a first date." The group muffles some laughter. "Shall we do some examples?" Some Descendants stand and tell lies, others tell the truth, Peter is right every time. Some blush at the embarrassment of the truth, others plop down in disappointment, leading to the next contestant with the same determination to fool the human lie detector.

Peter hunches forward under his light grey coat and murmurs short words, enough to please the crowd. His silent facade pushed for the entertainment of learning. His calm demeanour awkward and always listening, searching for the truth or the lie.

Next is Julius. He ditched the duster and wears a tight crewneck. My compliments to Onyx. "Hey, guys," He waves, exposing the muscles in his chest and perfectly aligned teeth. "So, I'm the least interesting Preceptor you have." Mock booing comes from the back row as Onyx sneaks away from her group and into the crowd.

Her black eyes appraise the group of Descendants on the ground and Brody calls her over. She struts, not caring that everyone else is sitting and she towers over us in her wedge heels. Her feet poke in the gaps of limbs and step on my fingers. I stifle a scream and yank them away, raising them to my mouth to breathe warm air on the pulsing pain of having them squished. "Oopsies. My bad." She crouches down next to me. "Caradoc ditched so I've been tormenting Julius for an hour." I stare at her, but don't ask.

Julius beams and continues on. "However, I'm the best study date you can ask for." He stares at Onyx as he speaks. "From process of elimination I hope you correctly assumed the category my affinity falls under. And for those who've lived here long and don't know it, I'm disappointed." Julius is outshone by the elder Preceptors and yet, he excels in the camp's Sense of Sight. "Before you ask, I do not see into the future or through people's clothes. I excel more in the better half, the knowledge. You've all come to this camp to better your Sight of Knowledge. I am here because I retain all the information I've learned since the first time I arrived at a camp and recall it at will. Anything I have read or learned is saved to my memory. My research allows me to excel in Sight because I can analyze and create distinctions based on darkness and light."

"More like human diction-FAIRY," Onyx hollers in a deep voice. Her disguise fails as Julius works to conceal his laughter and winks at her. I slump, blending into the Descendants around me to hide myself from any assumption that suggests we're friends.

Doctrine day continues until dinner. Caradoc doesn't return and Peter remains edgy. Zilla leads discussion, using the instructors as props in her skits. Julius proudly accepts insults from Onyx. Calix stares at me over the crowd of cross-legged Descendants, but doesn't come over.

Chapter 20

The Summoning is scheduled for next week during the Summer Solstice. The pit in my stomach grows, weighing down my thoughts and suppressing my appetite.

"What if they don't come?" I whisper the sentence that has been replaying in my mind since Doctrine Day.

"She will," Calix says, ignoring the idea of Jeremy.

He practices his shot and pierces the nose of the dummy. I sit on the floor, retiring an hour ago in exchange for a moment of self-pity. Calix hangs his bow and skips towards me with a bounce in his step.

"Hey, Belle, you'll reunite with her. I believe that if something were wrong and your sister needed help, you'd feel it—like an internal warning." He shrugs, crouching down to join me. He dusts the dirt on his pants and combs his messy black hair. It filters through his fingers before falling in front of his eyes. I draw circles in the sand of the arena floor.

"I think I'm more scared for if she comes. What do I say? How do I act?" Brett and Jeremy would stay in the region at a camp if Crystal deemed them strong enough for Sight. Next week they would attend the Summoning as a Descendant and I would have to face them after over a month of Sense exercises and emotional separation.

I wonder if I look the same.

Calix pulls on a loose curl. "They'll still love you. You will reunite with your sister. She wouldn't give up on you, either." He says the right thing. I frown, wanting to lean into the nook of his shoulder, but knowing I have to stop myself.

"Do you remember your parents?" I don't ask how he ended up at camp or about his time here. I have never invaded his personal history. Only collected bits and pieces of Meeting Square chatter. Arriving at camp at thirteen meant he would have some recollection of his early childhood. My chest flutters at the image of a small dark-haired boy causing trouble and running around, untamed like his messy hair.

"My dad left to fight. Didn't know my mother. He said I am expected to stay here, that there will come a day when this place will need me. Young at the time, I thought he had the greatest job of honour. And he would tell a story about this camp, probably to get me to stay." He laughs humourlessly. He lived here all these years as a duty to his father.

"What's the story?" I ask, not wanting him to stop.

"A broken bell that wouldn't sing. Its centre is inscribed with a secret that leads to a direct Descendant. And the day it cries out will lead the call for battle. One that will wage the war of balance, calling the angels back to Earth," Calix says, looking into the distance at the empty bleachers.

"And the bell?" I say.

"It's not here. I know every nook and secret passage of this camp. It doesn't exist. Just an old prophecy warriors pass on in battle to give them purpose. He got me to stay, he achieved his aim." I ache to hug him. Abandoned at a young age by his father, like Brett and me. I understand what he's feeling though mine is fresh. To continue to remain here even after knowing the story is untrue.

"Dads suck," I mutter.

"I think he believed he made the right choice. He was dedicated to his fight, noble even." Calix rises to his feet and I know the conversation about his past is over. His sarcastic smirk is back in its usual place and his eyes drain of emotion. "It's getting late."

I roll onto my hip and reach a hand up for assistance, but he's already climbing the bleachers.

Lara didn't intend to move in at first, her clothes were in a neat pile on the floor before I relocated them into my dresser. Cattia has slept over at Rachel's non-stop the past few weeks, which resulted in Lara bunking here most nights. With her room occupied by sneers and whispers, the safest place for her to sleep was in my room, one Cattia exchanged for Rachel's. Her brain sister was now missing a lobe and replacing it with boy talk and cheap gossip. Even Cattia's country posters somehow migrated down the hall. Thank God she took the horse clock with her.

After a week of sleeping in opposite beds, a silent exchange took place. Cattia packed up the last of her things and Lara did the same; they swapped dorms. Rachel swapped hairstyles. No one intervened.

Onyx found the new change inviting. She skipped knocking altogether and went for a more subtle barge, joining in until she felt tired. I was never formally introduced to Onyx's roommate, then again Onyx isn't exactly the most courteous. Her roommate never caused her problems, probably because Onyx isn't someone you want on your bad side.

"I'm not intimidating. I love Michelle!" Onyx says when we tell her she needs to respect curfew for both us and her roommate. It is past eleven and her heels slap against the stone floor of our dorm room.

"Her name is Sofia." I smack my face and frown.

"*Aunque la mona se vista de seda, mona se queda.*" Lara sighs from her corner. Her bedsheets alternate between blue and yellow polkadots.

"Exactly what Rosa said." Onyx rolls her R's and points to Lara, who rolls her eyes.

"I said, even if the female monkey dresses in silk, she will remain a female monkey." Lara shrugs. Onyx crosses the room for a high five. Lara rejects the offer for a nail file. Onyx spins to me. I don't budge. She drops her arm.

"We're not kicking you out, we're just saying you can't stay until 3:00 AM again." I soften my voice, coddling a child who cries in trouble.

"Please. You have Lara now. Way better than Cattia. She changed so quickly, thinking she's better than us with her annoying Southern drawl. Probably possessed by a demon." She snorts. "Rachel deserves it, if you ask me, ignoring you like that. Not cool, Lara. You were like frick and frack. Whatever that means." Onyx picks at the skin of her callused hands. Lara frowns, not yet in the angry phase of her best-friend break-up.

Cattia did change quickly. She went from Southern belle to anti-Christ real fast. What did they say resulted in a demon? That darkness uses people as hosts, it's often not obvious, and it is seen as a rebellious phase. Did she twitch or sweat a lot?

"Hellooo, Earth to Izzy? You want me to leave because you have a hot date?" Onyx pokes a sharp nail into my arm.

"I do not have a date. I'm just tired," I whine.

"Okay, so why's Calix here?" She points, and her red hair shimmers as she nods in the direction of the door.

Lara's on her feet, her comforter tossed over the edge of her bed in a messy heap. She holds the knob open in a dramatic reveal. Calix's broad shoulders fill the frame. His fists bunch in his pockets and he rolls onto his heels. He smirks, but his dark eyes are cautious. Unsure if the door is about to swing in his face or not. He waits for my command, one that can lead to either of his preplanned reactions. Resentment or approval.

"I, well, this is a surprise." My mouth goes dry. I glance at my oversized T-shirt and peeping cheeky underwear and throw a blanket around my waist. Onyx wiggles her eyebrows and leans on my bed.

"Well, well, well. To think you were a good girl, Izzy. You liar." She swivels a finger and pokes my nose. "You like the bad boys." I don't respond. She doesn't care. "Give me the details later. You kids behave, or don't. I want a good bedtime story." Her black eyes dance in amusement. She folds her legs into my bed and pulls the sheets to her neck. She fluffs the pillow and plops her head down.

Lara closes the door after I hold up a finger, requesting for a minute but unable to talk yet. Onyx dresses me with smutty commands from my mattress, which means my boobs are my main feature and my hair is unbrushed. I yank the door closed on her hollers and Lara's Spanish declarations of love.

"I want to show you something," Calix says. He leans against the opposite wall. The shadow from the fluorescent bulb casts a dark halo on his black hair.

I follow his direction, placing my feet lightly with the hope not to echo. He wanders in front, occasionally sneaking a backwards glance to make sure I'm still here. He leads me down the hall, through the Square, and to the train drop off.

We cross over the tracks into the forest.

Chapter 21

Calix heaves branches out of the way, guiding me through the trees despite the darkness. He hasn't spoken much, aside from the odd gruff order to watch my step or turn left. The air is cool for the middle of June. The moon casts a silver light through the leaves above. Fallen branches cover the dirt ground, swaying trees lean against the trunks of others, a breeze ruffles my hair and raises goosebumps along my forearms.

"Are we allowed to leave camp?" I never thought of it, sure there are rules in place and repercussions when you break them. Then again, sneaking out past curfew has become a regular part of my schedule, like arriving late to breakfast and groaning through Lara's screening of *The Notebook* every Friday night.

"I don't see a sign that says we can't." Calix hitches a foot over a moss blanketed trunk and swings himself over. I gawk—his movements are effortless. He lands with a silent, graceful step.

Already winded from the walk, I root my foot into the ground and place my other on the base of the fallen tree. I kick up from the dirt, push into the trunk and lunge forward. I wobble, unable to bring my other foot up. My fist connects with my chin and my jaw snaps shut, clenching my teeth together. The weight of my body falls with gravity. My shoe slips free and I plummet backwards. My tailbone connects with the packed ground and my butt imprints the soil. I huff, ducking to hide my face. A quick glance at Calix and I know he's seen.

His dark eyes sparkle in the moonlight and his lips purse together, his failed attempt at hiding his laughter. He reaches over the tree and tugs me to my feet. I swipe at my backside to release the dirt from the fabric of my pants. I rub at my tailbone and know I'll be walking funny tomorrow. Cue Onyx jokes now.

Calix hops over as smoothly as he leapt across before. He intertwines his fingers and hunches forward to offer me a step. I position my dirty shoe in his hands and he propels me upwards. I reach my toe onto the trunk and bring my other foot to join. I straighten up, basking in the view in front of me. Over the moss-covered trunk the ground slants downward. Thin grass grows waist-high and shimmers in the breeze. The trees thin, forming a clearing up ahead. The moon beckons us forward, a beacon against the grass, an active spotlight to the exit in front of us. I jump down and tread towards the break in the trees.

The clearing marks the end of the forest. A cliff mocks the idea of free land. The dirt reflects the moonlight above and twinkles like spilt glitter. Fog hangs in front of me. I reach forward, running my fingers through a wall of frosted droplets. Moist beads stick to my skin. The ripple of water below echoes up like a steady stream. I peer down, unable to determine how far the drop is. I squint forward, unsure how long the empty expanse stretches on.

Calix watches me from the tree line, not wanting to interrupt as I take in the void in front of me. The thick layer of mist clouds the unknown, blanketing me from the openness of freedom.

His footfalls are light, brushing against the dirt and circling to squat beside me. He swings his legs over the cliff edge and shuffles to help me. I plop down next to him. Why not, the pants are already ruined. I exhale a cloud of breath that gets lost in the fog. The cliff drops into nothingness.

"I come here to think." His deep voice sounds loud in the silence.

"Yeah, a smart guy like you has stuff to think about? I assumed you had it all figured out." I try to joke, but my voice comes out a whisper.

"When everyone wants a piece of you, you need to save a piece for yourself," he says. I listen for any trace of humour or sarcasm in his voice, but find none. The weight of his stare is heavy on my face. Fog morphs in circles and expands in sheets of air, hovering in stratum coats.

"Belle," he says. My stomach somersaults, climbing in my throat. I swallow it down. The crown of my hair dampens and my hands clam up. A weight on my chest makes it hard to breath.

He sweeps my curls over my shoulder, exposing my cheek to the moonlight. I inhale, pressing my nails into the dirt to steady myself. I glance up at him, my feet kicking into the side of the cliff in an offbeat, jittery motion. He twirls a curl, analyzing the puffy texture of my hair—the consequence of summer humidity. The moon casts a line of light down the bridge of his nose. He tilts his head, leaving half his face in shadow. His dark brown eyes look black against the sky above. The light reflects in his eyes and flickers like the glint of the stars in the sky. His hair swoops over his eyebrows, the strands in their usual muss. I trace the line of his jaw, and the stubble tickles my fingertips.

I can't separate the colours of his eyes as they deepen, hungrily, drinking in the feel of my skin as he rubs underneath the seam of my shirt along my lower back. His warm fingers trail over my waistband, not daring to explore anywhere else.

His breath flutters teasingly across my cheeks, our noses almost touching. His half-lidded eyes watch my mouth. His lips find mine, colliding softly and steering me in a deep rhythm. He searches my skin with eagerness as if exploding free from a binding restraint I didn't know he was under. His full lips squish, beckoning mine open to breath in my taste. The taut muscles in his chest rub against my cleavage. I trail my fingers under the thin fabric of his shirt and over his toned stomach.

He gasps from the coldness of my skin. Our bodies flare, heat throbbing from my chest to my cheeks as he unhooks my bra.

A snap of a twig sends us flying apart.

We shoot to our feet. I pat down my hair trying to tame the mess of my curls. Calix tucks in his shirt and adjusts the bulge in his pants. I re-hook the clasp of my bra.

"Ahem." He lets out a shaky breath and points at my chest.

My V-neck droops lower and exposes the crevice of my cleavage. I yank the collar up to my throat and swing my hair over the front of my shirt. Calix squints into the trees and holds a finger to his swollen lips.

He prowls forward, leaning as he rushes to the tree line. He positions himself low to the floor and signals me over. I mimic his run, but feel twice as stupid. He tilts his ear up, listening for a change of sound. Another branch cracks.

Calix takes off in a run. Soundless as his feet patter against the uneven ground. He leaps over the debris of the forest with ease. I maintain a steady pace, one that will allow me to stay quiet.

After minutes of stopping for air and cursing my heavy-set thighs, Calix finds me. He sneaks around a tree. With a raised hand he signals me to get down. I shoot him a glare. I've spent enough time in the dirt tonight, thank you.

I wiggle through branches and jutting out twigs until I'm behind him. I'm panting. Sweat beads my forehead and my cheeks flush. I place a palm on his back to steady myself. His lips turn up in a lopsided grin and I forget how to breathe completely. I shake my head, suppressing the memories of what took place a few minutes ago and willing myself to focus on the silhouettes amongst the trees.

Silver hair trembles furiously in frustration as a hushed conversation echoes in the trees. Caradoc. He growls what sounds like a warning. A hiss responds. It takes me a moment to realize he isn't speaking a familiar language. The obscured figure stands behind a tree out of view, strategically placed in the shadows to conceal itself from onlookers. What is Caradoc doing in the woods? What is he upset about? What the fuck kind of language is he speaking?

"We should go," Calix whispers. I give him a look, voicelessly asking, "And miss the good part?" He nods towards the figures in the trees. Goosebumps lift the hairs on my neck and I shiver. *It's not safe.* He signals.

We track our original route and I find myself wondering why we didn't skip the large moss-covered trunk on the way over. An unnecessary obstacle doesn't make for a short cut. Somehow Calix keeps us on track, shimmying through trees and pulling me after him, never letting go of my hand. Now, this would be a form of flattery if his tall strides matched mine. Leaves and twigs sweep against my exposed skin and tug my hair the whole way.

We find ourselves at the train tracks behind Residence. I grip my knees, crouch down and gulp a breath of air, holding a finger at his face. I won't specify which finger it is. Calix smirks, amusement etches the wrinkled lines around his mouth and forehead. He grabs my finger and motions to bite it, but settles for a nibble. I pull it free, but he refuses to refrain from touching me, settling for subtle hair tugs and pokes as we stroll the length of the rectangle building.

I push open the doors of Residence, expecting to see an upset Preceptor on duty. The desk is empty. The chair swiveled towards the door as if someone left in a hurry. Calix circles the desk and lifts a page from the messy heap. He shrugs, not knowing what it means.

Calix escorts me to my bedroom door. We don't talk the whole way, not wanting to risk someone overhearing. I grip the door knob, waiting for a protest not to open it. His fingers wrap my forearm and he spins me to face him. He tilts so his mouth is only a few inches away from mine.

"Oh, no you don't!" Onyx yanks the door open behind me and I tumble in. Calix is stunned for a moment, but recovers into his usual cocky smirk.

"Goodnight, Belle," he croons, trotting down the hall and away from Onyx's spitfire. I groan as she shoves me towards the bed.

"What the fuck was that? Are y'all spit buddies now?" Her red hair is wound in a tight bun, making her look more like an angry teacher than a concerned friend. "Do I have to give you the talk about protection or are you smart enough for that? No disrespect to your momma, I'm sure she's watching from the Heavens and loving a grandchild, but does he even know what he wants in his future? How are you going to reach balance with a distraction? Finish school. Then you can date." She nods, happy with her logic.

I plop my head into my hands and stare at her through the spaces in my fingers. "It was just a kiss!" I whine.

"So you did kiss?" Onyx sits beside me. "How was it?" I stare at her, then look at Lara for help. She yawns and rubs her eyes, woken up by Onyx's shrill voice. Either she waited up like a concerned parent or a curious friend—she needs to pick one. My mind spins with a replay of the night.

"Good... *Really* good," I say.

"Not too good I hope. I wasn't kidding about the protection talk. I'm sure the camp has supplies somewhere." She aims towards the door as if planning to get me condoms right now.

"Please don't. Nothing happened!" I say.

"You just said you kissed. And that it was good." She gives me a pointed look, trying to catch me in a lie.

"Onyx, I'm a virgin!" I yell, throwing myself onto my pillow. Her mouth opens and Lara glances vacantly between us, as if trying to piece together what is going on.

Onyx motions the sign of the cross. "Oh, thank Baby J. I didn't know with a body like yours. I was sure men wanted a better look." She rushes towards me, kneeling beside my bed and flattening my hair as she pets me with frantic strokes.

"Like my mother used to say, *ojo que no ve, corazón que no siente*. What you don't know can't hurt you." Lara's mattress creaks as she shuffles to get comfortable. She throws the covers over herself.

"Except an unplanned pregnancy," Onyx mutters.

No one mentions Jeremy and my chest contracts with guilt. I want to roll in a ball and let Onyx give me one of her lectures about the importance of DTR, determining the relationship. I don't even know what Jeremy and I are anymore. A relationship two best friends fell into and never questioned. I replay the kiss in my mind and turn onto my stomach. Onyx sifts through Lara's drawers, searching for something to wear. Lara tosses in her bed and yawns. Her eyes blink as they adjust to the lamplight. She catches Onyx in the act.

They bicker over a denim mini-skirt. It stretches like a flag between them. Their friendship, so familiar to me, reminds me of how Jeremy and I were before Mom died. I ask myself the question no one does. What about Jeremy?

After a bargain of heels for the miniskirt, the two settle into boy talk. Eventually, Onyx leaves remembering our 3:00 AM agreement.

I don't tell them I saw Caradoc in the woods; I don't mention the woods at all.

I refuse to let myself tear apart the sweet moment with Calix. But Onyx's questions planted the seed. I lay, staring at the stone ceiling, doubting if the kiss even happened. The moon leaves lines of silver light on my wall through the shutters of my blinds. He did unhook my bra with ease. Maybe he's more experienced. What would have happened if we weren't interrupted? Would I have given in to temptation? Does he even like me? I replay the moment over in my mind until it shuts off.

I fall asleep to a vivid dream of a smouldering forest and a kiss.

Chapter 22

My sister arrives today. I throw my bedsheets on the floor, then think better of it and bend to pick them back up. I flip my duvet and tuck it in tight around the mattress. I stuff my clothes pile into the drawers and battle to brush down my curls. I switch my training outfit for one more casual. My shipment of clothes and Onyx's credit card has filled my closet to normal capacity.

Onyx meets Lara and me in the hall outside our door. Our trip down to the Square is quiet as we prepare to meet the other Descendants. No one says that Brett and Jeremy may not attend another regional camp. No one says that they might have rejected balance. No one says that their bodies may not have accepted Sight. No one says that they are weak. No one says that they aren't coming. No one says my fears. No one says anything.

Calix combs a curl as he passes, a secret caress in the crowd of Descendants. He moves to join Julius against the wall of instructors. I link arms with Onyx and Lara. Ash and Brody stand behind us. I rise on my tiptoes for a better view of the train tracks. Onyx lifts her chin; her stilettos and long legs are an unfair advantage. Bodies exit Doctrine and Ordnance, joining us in the Meeting Square to greet the other camps. A gold banner hangs across the square announcing the Summer Solstice Summoning. Its strings are wound from the exit tunnels of Doctrine as it droops and flutters overhead. I'm sure Zilla's doing.

A hum of whispers vibrates through the Square. Excitement courses through everyone as they list friends they met during previous Summonings and guess the names called to duty this year. The buzz of laughter stings my ears and does little to soothe my growing nerves.

A train horn sounds in the distance and the ground rumbles. The voices are hushed beneath the loud vibration of the tracks as the wheels trot closer. The train yields to a screeching stop. The Meeting Square rings with silence. I hold my breath. The Preceptors step forward. The swoosh of opening doors echoes, then they thud into their slits, one by one, across the length of the train.

Then Descendants pour out and the crowd cheers in welcome. Blurs of purple, blue, brown, black and blond hair approach then sink into the people around me. My heart tightens and I drop my friends' arms, ignoring them as they call out my name. Brett. She has to come. My sister. She has to come here. Brett. Where is she? My sister. She's alive. My pulse thuds in my ears, a rhythm of her name on repeat.

"Isabelle!" Her voice breaks through the muffled crowd. Hearing my name is like a lungful of air after being submerged underwater for too long.

I push aside the limbs of bystanders, unsure if they go to camp or are visitors. I shift my body sideways and squeeze, thinning myself to fit through tightly wound embraces. Old friends pat each other's back and position their arms for a hug. I cut through their gestures of homecoming welcome like an arrow thrown to its target.

I shove until I'm free. The air envelopes my chest, filling my lungs and releasing the pressure in my eyes. Tears pool over and the stray wisps of curls stick to my wet cheeks.

"Brett," I whisper.

She leans forward, holding herself back from a run. Her highlighted hair outgrew, exposing her blonde roots. The blue in her eyes is lighter, like how they usually are in the summer.

Her nails are chewed and her lips crack in a smile. We collide, a hug that lasts a minute and binds the days apart. We absorb the weight of each other's absence and drink in the fears of solidarity until they relinquish. She's alive. My sister, she's safe.

Chapter 23

The Meeting Square is set up with extra benches to accommodate our visitors. Brett sits at our table, describing her camp and comparing the buildings. She says they are aligned in the same format, but in different stone. Where everything here is the washed-out colour of brown sand, hers is a rocky grey. She introduces me to a few friends, one with green hair and another with tight braids fastened against her scalp. Brett dismisses herself to test our fighting gear.

"Be safe!" I call after her, smiling as she bolts through the Square. A month ago I would have cut her myself if I found out she was playing with knives.

"Awe, look, the baby bird left its nest, how heartwarming." Cattia snickers to Rachel as she passes.

"I think you mean heart-worming, like the two of you, and I don't appreciate you preying on my friends. You're standing too close, pesky mosquito. Bye." Onyx creates a shooing motion and Cattia sneers. I raise my eyebrows and Onyx shrugs and licks yogurt from her spoon, finding sense in her comeback.

"Isabelle?" Someone gasps behind me.

Lara whistles. Cattia and Rachel gawk, half-raised from the neighbouring bench. Jeremy stands, eyebrows pinched together, hiding his hands in his pockets. His broad shoulders are leaner through his muscle shirt than I remembered. His once-cropped hair hangs over the brim of his forehead, shorter than Calix's, but longer than I last saw. His brown eyes are soft and his square jaw relaxed.

"Jeremy!" I leap into his arms before I can think about the motion. I'm filled with the familiar memory of his body against mine in moments of reassuring hugs and late-night movies. I inhale and stiffen. The smell of his mom's cooking and freshly mowed grass is gone. The squishiness of his body is replaced with a layer of muscle. His voice hardened in the time we spent apart.

I step away, dropping my arms to my side. His face is neutral, the longing in his eyes replaced with a sadness. I know it now. We've changed. We were different long before we left for camp, but we latched onto each other. He acted as the father figure Brett needed and I filled the closeness he never received in his own home. Our need for companionship and family replaced the need for love.

"You look good." His lips curl upward, relaxed like always. It's the same grin that I've known since I was seven when he crossed the schoolyard and invited me to his birthday. I was the only girl there. He gave me my own decorated sugar cookie so I wouldn't have to eat his blue Power Ranger cake. The birthday invitation is still wedged in a box somewhere at Aunt Jo's.

"You, too." My throat is tight.

"I'll see you around, Isabelle." He leans in to kiss my temple. My tears well up and pressure surfaces behind my eyes. I turn around, staring at my plate of pancakes while Onyx leans on Lara fanning herself.

I'm about to sit when I notice a head of black hair charges the tunnel of Ordnance. Calix.

I abandon my plate and rush after him, reaching for his clenched fists and prying apart his fingers and lacing them with mine. He refuses to look at me, but I can see his brown eyes are clouded with anger. He flexes his jaw and I trail my fingers against his cheeks, smoothing down the hard lines of his face.

"Calix. Will you stop?" He pushes past me.

"Leave me alone, Belle. Go reunite with your family and rekindle your love with your boyfriend. Life's a fairytale for you, right? Everything works out, everyone loves Isabelle. You get to leave and I'm stuck here," he says, mocking me with a girl-pitched voice.

"You can leave to." I frown.

"No, I can't." He laughs dryly. "I owe it to my father. He left me here, didn't come back. I knew him, he didn't do that because he gave up on his only son. Something happened to him. It's my duty to listen to his final request." Calix raises his voice, looming over me and jabbing each word into my memory.

He's lived here for ten years, of course he imagined reuniting with his father. He had to imagine the day his father came back for him. Had to replay the moment his father left over and over in his mind. Had to dwell over whether he was abandoned, forgotten or struck by a tragedy. He had to stay, because his father would know where he left him and come back one day.

"Calix," I start. He brushes past me.

"I have to go." He disappears into the darkness of the hall until I can no longer make out the blackness of his hair.

We crowd around the wooden table for dinner and Calix is nowhere in view. Jeremy isn't here, either. Of course I don't think they're brawling somewhere, but maybe Calix stuffed Jeremy in a ditch.

"So, I'm in second level Touch, some say my affinity will make me an awesome warrior one day. I was sent to the camp for being weak in Touch and I'm already getting the hang of it." Brett stabs a slice of roast beef with her fork and eats it like a Popsicle. Onyx nods, impressed.

"You are safe, right? No running into danger without seeing a clear route out. Remember what Crystal said?" I scold.

"Yeah, I've been getting a lot of one-on-one training with

Derek. He says I'm progressing quickly." Brett shrugs, seeing no threat for imbalance.

"Derek?" I ask. Brett rolls her eyes, wolfing down another piece of meat.

She's grown taller over the past month. The chubbiness in her cheeks disappeared into the rest of her slender frame. She has to do something with that hair of hers. I yank at her split ends, laugh and squeeze her into me. Despite her protests I hug her harder.

"Eeesh, relax, Izzy. Before you suffocate her with your boobs." Onyx points a fork at me.

Brett slept in the visitor wing of Residence last night. I hate having her so close, but not able to keep an eye on her. We crowd the Square and Brett waits for us at our usual table. She's quick, I'll give her that.

She holds up a thin arm, blocking a hug attack from forming. I frown and she pats my shoulder. Onyx presses her lips together to keep from laughing. Zilla steps through the centre hall of Doctrine, her oil-black coat gliding over the sandy ground.

"Descendants," she calls through the expanse. The early morning chatter silences. "Another attack took place late last night." She hangs her head. Julius and Peter are at her flanks, their chins held high, their faces blank.

I search the Square for Calix. Jeremy catches my eye and waves. No bruising or scrapes visible. I exhale. Tensing again, when I realize Calix is avoiding me. Real mature. I wiggle on the bench, trying to focus on Zilla's words.

I don't recognize the name of the person who died last night. Brett gasps. She forms the sign of the cross and lowers her head, mouthing a short prayer I've never heard her say. The attacks have spread to different camps. I gulp, wanting to clutch Brett's arm and tug her to my body. Instead I swap for thrumming my fingers against the table. A look from Onyx cuts the beat short.

"As Descendants it is our duty to protect those who

cannot protect themselves. We have honour in defending the imbalanced, however, we forget that as Descendants we need protection, as well. For those of you who have not found their affinity or excelled, you are imbalanced. In not admitting that, you dismiss your Sight." Zilla pauses, fixing her gaze on individual Descendants in the crowd. The air is thick as we hold our breaths, waiting for her next words. "Our transition to balance is our most vulnerable. The scale can fall either way. It is our duty to defend each other and harness our power. With knowledge we can eliminate the weakness pled by ignorance. In our strength we generate a force against the darkness in our kind. In the truth of our purpose we can unite against the darkness. And today we find reason. Look amongst yourselves, at the familiar faces around you, the friends and family who you have missed, and those you have grown to love here." I glance from Brett, her blue eyes as familiar as my own, to Onyx and Lara, whose sass have caused me to laugh my way through homesickness.

"Someone today has lost a person dear to them. Do what you can to make sure it will not happen to you." Brett scoots closer and touches her leg to mine. "Now, as a Preceptor I must remind you that we—" she gestures to Julius and Peter. "—are not superior to you. We have taken an oath to God to pledge that we will not limit the resources we can afford to provide. We devote ourselves to your balance to ensure that, if you choose, you can one day act in our role and succeed." Her voice is empty of emotion. "With the utmost unease, I regret to inform you all that you are in danger." The silence hangs in the Square like a blade over its victim. We wait, readying ourselves for a challenge or for her to burst into laughter and admit she tells a cruel joke. But if there's anything I know, it's that Zilla doesn't joke. I don't think she laughs, either.

My back straightens and my palms sweat. Murmurs start to spread across the tables as Descendants ask each other what she means, if she's telling the truth, if it's a result of imbalance, if there's a reason why so many of us are dying. Zilla waits. Julius stands frozen, his face stern and his stare forward. Peter scans the crowd with furrowed brows, never resting on someone long enough for me to read his expression.

"I cannot withhold truth from you, for it will leave you at a grave risk. Knowledge is key to Sight and preparation." Another pause. "Now you all know our Summoning has been rescheduled to dispatch new Descendants more rapidly. We need the bodies—the warriors, the teachers, the protection. As our camps expand we will welcome new friends, but as we have you now, we will allow you the honesty to pass on to them. The attacks are becoming more frequent, which means we need a collective of Descendants to hold post. The Summoning will provide immediate warriors and dispatch Exorcists to regional towns to provide immediate assistance. We do not know the extent of the force we are dealing with, only that is it not a coincidence that we have lost so many in such short time. We will not act as the host for anything but the angel in our bloodline. I look forward to seeing you all at the Summoning tomorrow." Zilla spins on her heels, her black duster flapping behind her like a cape, concealing her in the shadows of Doctrine.

The Square erupts. Some girls cower in fear and hug each other, hanging from the necks of their friends and family. Others rush towards Ordnance to grab the closest weapon.

Onyx picks at her nails. "So, no breakfast or what?" The tables lie bare, not a single ceramic plate visible. The smell of fresh waffles and pancake batter absent. No crispy bacon, or grape vine to nibble. My stomach rumbles.

"We can go watch *The Notebook*," Lara suggests.

"No!" the table yells in unison.

Chapter 24

The sun is warm against my neck. Sweat beads along my hairline, causing loose curls to stick to the wet skin of my forehead and drips of perspiration to catch in the saggy skin under my eyes. I stayed up all night. No, I did not wait for Calix in Ordnance. I skipped the pity party and didn't go. In fact, I relocated it to my dorm. He wasn't invited.

Brett plumps down next to me on the bench at breakfast, leaving Onyx tapping her wedge heels. It's not long before Onyx kicks Ash and Brody to another table to sit down. She gives a sidelong glance at Brett, but doesn't say anything, leaving me to deal with my sister's lack of courtesy the way a mother is expected to scold her child. Instead I ask Brett about camp.

"No, Jeremy isn't there with me." My chest squeezes at the thought of her alone for the past month. She's twelve and already living on her own. Mom wouldn't even let me check the mailbox last summer when I was nineteen.

"Jeremy is so fiiiine. Isabelle, how do you do it? Him and Calix!" Lara asks. Onyx motions towards her chest, cupping at invisible air.

"Calix?" A deep voice asks behind me. I swivel around to find Jeremy balancing a tray of bacon and a cup of orange juice.

"Oh, hey, Jer," I give Lara a warning look, signaling her not to say another word.

Even though the separation didn't cause for a romantic reunion or a spill of emotions, we still haven't talked about where this leaves our relationship. Some would assume that time apart would make our relationship stronger. That discovering a part of your past is something to bring you closer to those bonds already forged deeply in your life. That the truth will provide better understanding of life and appreciation for love. Those same people would also call you a Bible Freak when you say you descend from an angel.

"Just came by to say good luck to everyone at the Summoning today." He nods, reaching to rub Brett's hair. His bulky arms stick out from another muscle shirt and expose the now flat side of his torso. I'll have to ask him about his style choice, too.

"So, who do you think the Preceptors will Summon to duty? Anyone you know?" Brett chirps and the table continues to point at strangers, guessing at their imagined affinity and excelled Sense. I gaze after Jeremy. I fork at the stack of pancakes on my plate. I'm no longer hungry.

The dome is separated into different regions. I scan the crowd for Brett's blonde ponytail, but hope to glimpse a head of dishevelled black hair instead. Where is he? I lean on the edge of the bleacher, half-sitting as I squint at the roomful of Descendants. Onyx watches me from the corner of her eye. I shake my head. *Don't ask.*

A whine rumbles in Ash's chest like a strained breath. Onyx glances down to me again and I nod. *You ask.* We turn to Ash. "You okay there, pops?" Onyx nudges his shoulder. He doesn't move, staring at the ceiling. His face reddens and his hands clench. I wait for a witty comeback and when it doesn't come I conclude the search for my sister and focus on the pair of bulging green eyes next to me. "Ash?" Oynx asks, her voice a pitch higher. "Breathe, dammit!" She shakes his arm, but he continues to sit straight, unmoving despite the strength of her shove. His whole body is stiff like the stone bench, unable to break his trance.

"What is it?" I whisper. I cup his arm. His skin is slick with a layer of sweat.

"Hear. Something." He grunts, still not breathing.

I listen. Nothing but excited chatter answers me. The Summoning hasn't started yet as Zilla gathers the instructors and Preceptors from other camps. I try to read Ash's face for more information, but Onyx frantically shakes him.

"What do you hear? Are there too many sounds?" Onyx shoots out questions like a fresh round of ammunition. She wheels towards me. "Do you think his affinity is sensitive when he's surrounded by a large group of people? We've never been in a room this crowded."

"No." Ash's voice is dry as his throat expands. "Listen."

Onyx rubs his shoulders as if warming him would help. I knead my temples. "Not a good time to nap, Izzy!" Onyx says, her voice bordering hysterics.

I let go of the surrounding chatter. The room falls silent as I enter my mind into the familiar exercise I practice at the end of Sound class with Aliza. First comes the rumble of voice, then rustle of leaves, and farther out the ripple of water. My ears work to peel through the geographic layers of sound. I stretch my sense past the camp and the shallow noise, searching for a message in the rhythm of the wind. I follow the force of air that drives the rotation of all motions. The inhalation of breath as words flow from lips, the breeze that sweeps through the trees, the push of waves that channels the stream.

Then I hear it. A shriek that pierces my ears and causes me to squeeze my eyes shut. Onyx's command is lost in the sound of wind. My hair rocks and swings in the strong current. The warning the same as the one I heard when I first arrived at camp. I fight through the shallow sounds, blocking out pieces of conversation and dig through the layers of distraction to reach the surface of the cry. The room falls to a hush as the pressure snaps.

Go to him. The wind whispers in my ear.

I rise to my feet, knowing exactly who the warning is for. I rush up the bleachers of the dome, taking the stairs two at a time. A cry splits through the chatter of voices. Someone in the audience falls forward in pain. I glance back, forcing my legs to lunge forward. Fair-hair curtains the face of a lanky frame. Mary-Anne snarls from the centre of huddled Descendants.

I don't stop.

Calix.

I bang my fists against the door of his dorm, fiddle the knob and kick the bottom. I lean an ear against the wood, listening for movement on the other side. When nothing changes I sprint down the hall, knowing one other place he could be.

I leap over the train tracks and break through the forest line. I swat the branches away from my face. Leaves claw at my cheeks. Twigs slap against my palms. Tree roots litter the dirt, breaking free from the solid ground and snatching at my ankles. It's too late to map out another path as I steer for the moss-covered trunk. I hitch up my heels and prepare a running start. I aim for the flat surface of the abandoned tree. My calves tighten and my legs pull as I vault over.

The ground slopes downward, encouraging me farther as I shoot through the tall grass. The cliff edge juts out into a thick wall of fog. I spin, stuck with the decision of left or right. I pick right, propelling myself into the mist cloud. I steady my pace and search the ground. It's all that is visible through the grey blanket of droplets. The forest around me blurs into a black shadow, wrapping the length of the cliff. What if he's the other way, I'm wasting time.

The cold air pierces my lungs and burns my nose. My throat expands and gulps thirsty breaths. My hair whips behind me, catching the wind in tethered knots. My chest rises, my pulse quickens, my eyes water. I don't slow down.

Slack feet and twisted limbs poke from the bottom of the fog blanket. My feet shuffle, my mouth opens, my hands pat against the dirt. I crouch to my knees and trail my fingers against his dark jeans and rub my palms along his black T-shirt. A sack of arrows lies tossed against the wrinkled trunk of a tree. His crossbow has been disposed of on top of a rock. Broken arrows spill across the sand. Their shafts split into sharp wooden stakes. I sweep back his wet hair. It's matted with dew. A shade of glossy black.

A swollen gash lines his temple. Dried brown liquid coats his forehead and trails down to his eyebrow. Blood. His lashes brush against his cheekbones. His plush pink lips are purple. His skin the colour of fog. An arrow wet with his blood.

I heave his shoulders into my lap and rest his head on my chest. The weight of his body is cold on mine. I want to scream, shake him awake, and call him an asshole all at once. A sob sounds from around me and rain drips on his cheeks. No one else is here. No one else can help. I'm crying.

My pants soak up the water from the wet sand. The wind rushes around me and rustles the trees. Leaves shake together in mock applause. Clouds rumble and start to spit. I shuffle under the weight of his body. My mind remains numb as I shift his slack arm around my neck and drag him into the tree cover. My feet inch forward, my heart waits at the camp. I have to bring him to safety. I have to help him. He's okay. He is.

If my muscles protest I don't hear them. I don't hear anything aside from the pulse in my ears as my heart works to digest what is happening. I don't feel anything aside from Calix's cheek slick with sweat on my neck as I loll his body up the hill, over branches and through the Meeting Square. I don't know where to go.

I push through the tunnel of Ordnance and shove his body forward. The wall supports us as we tumble down the stairs and into the dome. Our clothes stick to our skin, unsure if it's from rain or sweat. My nails dig into the skin above his hip as I struggle to grip him on the steps. The dip of the stairs causes the dead weight of his body to collapse on top of me. My elbow connects with the stone wall. I swear. The light from the gym grows near.

We enter the arena. The room explodes in shouts of command and wails of pain. Bleachers are full of hectic Descendants as they sling fists at each other. Groups of bodies cage in those transformed by darkness. An uproar of chaos echoes around us. The clang of sharp blades reverberate upward as they clash together. Blood splats the brown stone bleachers. The smell of sweat and rust wrinkles my nose. Everything erupts in motion as Descendants chase and defend one another.

Julius appears at my side with wild eyes. His ponytail flings out behind him.

"What happened? Isabelle? What happened?" He repeats his question. I'm unsure how many times he asks. My teeth are clenched shut under the weight of Calix's body.

"Found him," I grunt. My voice is hoarse from crying.

Julius slings his arm around Calix's waist and relieves me of half his weight. I refuse to let go of him and Julius doesn't ask me to. We shuffle Calix's slack body down the steps and into the weapons room. Descendants grab knives and batons off the wall in the rush of battle. No one notices as we throw Calix into a bath of murky water and plunge his body deep under the surface. We cradle him there.

I don't hear the questions Julius fires at me and I don't ask my own. I stare at the water and hold my breath as I wait. I don't breathe, measuring how long his body can go without air and as punishment for letting something happen to him. My pulse pounds, fighting against every breath I don't take. Forty-five… Forty-seven… Fifty-one… Nothing.

Julius stares, his expression grave, waiting for the boy he raised to resurface from the tub. I turn to grab a knife off the wall, readying to throw myself in war and stab someone. Whoever did this has to pay. They can't escape. Darkness doesn't win. You can't raise a generation telling them if you share, and smile, and say thank you, that the good will always prevail. It is bullshit.

The water splashes against my legs. I circle, reaching for the crown of black hair as it breaks free from the water.

Calix gasps and falls back, slipping into the tub and flinging out his arms. Julius and I grab for his wrists and place them on the brim of the small healing pool to help him balance. He tromps out of the water, splatting the ground with the heaviness of his jeans. The wet fabric of his clothes stretch flat against his body. His hair sticks to his face. A harsh pink line stretches from his eyebrow to his temple, a faint reminder of the wound. All traces of blood washed away with the memory of the gash.

Calix's brown eyes widen as he stares at the floor. His teeth chatter and Julius throws him a towel. I cross my arms and wait. Julius does the same. Calix gulps for air to calm his heavy breathing. He rubs a finger along his temple, feeling the bump in his skin from the new blemish. He drops his hand in a fist, clenches his jaw and flares his nostrils. His eyes darken and his brows sink.

"Caradoc," Calix says. Julius and I nod.

A harsh wind echoes through the tunnel in a scream. Descendants cover their ears. My hair whips around me like a banner. Julius' ponytail flutters from his shoulders and Calix's bangs blow back and expose his scar. Caradoc marches across the arena floor with his brown duster flapping behind him. His silver hair ruffles from the rush of the air and his hands stay rooted at his side. Unbothered by the shriek, Caradoc sneers. Behind his glasses his eyes are wild with the defiance of war.

"Descendants!" he greets. "You don't have to defend the new order. Balance is not purity! It is both darkness and light. Bring back the way of true harnessed power. Do not ignore your blood!" His voice booms through the bleachers and rings with the persuasion of someone who has an affinity in speech-giving from excelling in Voice of Reason. Descendants straighten, drinking in his words with the same thirst they had shown for battle against those who have changed. Always honouring the call to duty and ready to defend their blood's purpose.

"Balance isn't ejecting the darkness from your veins, but learning to live with it. How will you achieve light if there is no dark? What allows you to recognize your enemy and defend yourself is the part of the demon that lives on inside of you — your darkness. You are a part of your opponent and that's what makes it fair. In the new order balance became the fight against one or the other, against those who become one with the wrong side. There are two pieces of balance. Do not rid yourselves of the part that provides you strength for the promise of goodness. The angels fell so we could live in sin. The same sins they committed when they were exiled from Heaven." Caradoc's voice rises as his speech draws on. His accent harsh as he sings the song of war. Descendants look at one another. Unsure if they should act against a Preceptor or their training.

"You expect Descendants to reject lightness in exchange for darkness because it is of abundance?" I blurt. The bleachers are silent, everyone waits. Calix places a hand on my shoulder. His strength generates through to me. My feet square in a defensive stance, level with Caradoc's. I welcome a challenge.

"Yes, Isabelle." Caradoc's smile turns lethal as he prowls closer to me. Calix's hand flexes and a low growl rumbles in his chest. "I believe we can receive strength from both. To exist with our demons. Balance should not exist as the war between good and evil. There is sin in all of us and as our lineage runs shallow with each generation of Descendants, the darkness grows stronger. We can harness that darkness and convert ourselves into true warriors, a greater force with the Sight of our past. We will transform into the superior race not the silent guards of humanity." He bends his face down, and his body hovers over me. Spit flies from his lips as he speaks. His grey eyes bore into mine. "Our camps taught Descendants how to live with both sides of balance and to resurrect those who surrendered to full darkness. We did not reject them. The new order ruined that. Your mother was once on my side, long ago."

"My mom?" I whisper. Movement shuffles through the bleachers and the sound of footfalls echoes closer. I risk a glance past Caradoc. Mary-Anne, her eyes black and her skin grey, twitches as she snarls. Behind her, more Descendants with the same dark eyes and charcoal skin flank around Caradoc. Onyx would reject darkness just for the style limitations.

"She believed balance is composed of two. That darkness could exist in power without the demon. That we could learn to tame diluted bloodlines and harness it for new found strength. Until she met your stupid human father and thought she could hide from me!" he shouts. "We wanted to rebuild the new order into liberty, to restructure exercises to focus on more prominent blood. To publicize camps and regain our ranks on Earth as true Descendants. To live with darkness. Then she rejected her Summoned duty. She left. To live in secret rather than create change, that bitch." He prowls closer.

Mom, her blond hair and blue eyes innocent, even with every yell I threw at her in frustration over misplacing my favourite bag, running late for dance class or undercooking the chicken. Her patience through any struggle always left me with a pit of guilt and envy. She would cook her way out of anything with warm, melted chocolate chip cookies. The kind that stringed as you pulled them apart. How she would grit her teeth in traffic when we were late for school because she wouldn't dare go above the speed limit with Brett or me in the car. Her hugs came just as quickly as the tears in moments of weakness. Mom, a Summoned Descendant?

"I must admit, it took me awhile to track her down in Feathercoe. So close to camp, too. The satisfaction of finding the person who betrayed you and hearing them beg for their life. Mmmmm." He closes his eyes, as if tasting the memory. My mouth goes dry. Calix's arm flexes. "Then your idiot father had to get in the way. Told him to leave and I'd let you and your sister live. But like I said, there is sin in all of us. And, dear, I lied." His face morphs into a grotesque sneer. He reaches for my throat. His nails clawing for my skin. A flash of silver thrusts towards my stomach and I flinch, waiting for the impact and pain to burst through me.

Caradoc's feet are knocked out from under him. He flies and collapses against the floor. The force sends his followers tumbling around him. Zilla glides down from the bleachers. Her hand rises, calling her affinity to shove Caradoc away from me. His knife clatters to the stone ground of the weapon room. The dark Descendants round on Zilla, ready to protect their wicked leader and defend the attack against him.

The bleachers erupt in a call for battle as camp Descendants rush forward with their weapons drawn. Calix grabs a sack of arrows and fastens a strap across his chest. He puts a hand on me, his brown eyes frowning, longing to tell me things, but knowing it's not the time, or goodbye.

He lifts an arrow and it pierces the heart of an approaching demon. His smirk in place, he says, "Any chance I can convince you to sit this one out?"

"And miss real-life practice? Heck no." I remember the lecture Onyx gave me on the train when I first arrived about saying the word Hell. I search the crowd as a shimmer of red hair drop kicks someone in the chest. Oliver steals a shaft from his opponent with his mind. Lara dances around fists. Ash utilizes his affinity by hearing the advance of an attacker. He spins, swinging full force.

"Thought so." Calix pinches my chin and pulls it upward. His lips are soft and warm on mine. "Stay close to me and remember what I taught you." He slides a cool handle into my grasp. I examine the throwing blade, tossing it up to feel the weight. Oh yeah, this is good.

Calix sprints into the crowd of Descendants, his crossbow raised as an arrow sings through the air and punctures someone's thigh. I race after him. A charcoal skinned forearm stretches to clothesline my neck. I duck, but my nose still connects with the bone and I stumble backwards. Clotheslined on my first run to battle. I look up. Rachel, her recently dyed blonde hair now covered in a film of grey. She tilts her head and curls her lip at me the way a cat would stare at her prey. Calix whips around, jamming his elbow into the crook of her neck. She falls forward and I pull him after me.

My mind races to catch up with my feet. Rachel is a follower? Who else? Calix pulls me up the steps. I drop his hand and face the mess of the gym floor as bodies hunch over in injury. Blood paints the brown sand, changing it to the colour of rust. "Where's Brett?"

A pain shoots up my forearm as a spear slices through the muscle. I cry out, reaching at the open gash to stop the bleeding. Caradoc prowls closer. His grey eyes glint with humour from taking me off-guard. He lifts up his blade, challenging me to a fair duel.

"I knew you were the bell destined to start the motion of change, it was in your mother's blood, too. A silent Force. And to my satisfaction, the prophecy never says who wins." He jabs his spear at my heart.

Zilla pounces onto the bench in front of me. "You will not put my Descendant's in anymore danger. Surrender yourself before you lose your Sight." She raises her hand, willing her powers as a Transport.

"You always thought this was your camp because you excel in a greater force, but look at what my affinity has led to!" Caradoc opens his arms wide.

"Your fight of pure balance means good should still exist inside of you." Zilla flings a free rock from the ground and Caradoc deflects it. He swings his spear around his torso and helicopters it above his head, aiming the blade towards Zilla's side. She deflects the blow, channeling the spear away with air as it clips her hip. She grunts.

"Get out of here!" Zilla commands me. Calix grabs my arm and yanks me away.

Calix pushes me forward and stops to aim an arrow at someone behind us just as Rachel climbs up the bleachers. Her nails flex in bloody claws. She pulls Cattia by the neck and steadies her like a human shield. Cattia's cherry lips mouth a plea. Her blonde curls are flattened in a heap of sweat and crusted blood. Rachel squishes Cattia's windpipe more. She gasps for air and Rachel cackles.

Rachel's betrayal to Cattia mirrors the one Lara fought the past few weeks. Rachel's greying hair hangs between the transition of black to blonde, as if she lost the balance of light when deciding her friends. Her green eyes are so similar to Lara's that I fumble, unsure how I am supposed to fight her when a month ago she welcomed me to camp. Caradoc said we can resurrect darkness and save each other. Onyx once told me a demon cannot be undone. Mom believed there was a way. Cattia gasps for air, cutting off my reverie as Rachel stops her breathing. Cattia's fingers fumble at the charcoal skin of Rachel's arm.

Often, someone tries to save the person from the demon instead of realizing they're no longer separate entities and killing it.

The throwing knife feels heavy. Its weight places a strain on my shoulders. The warmth of the handle pulses with the quick beat of my heart. My palms sweat. The cut through my muscle burns. I don't imagine failure, only the destined root of the blade and my target. I lunge forward, leaning my body with the toss of the thin blade. It flies through the air and pierces Rachel's forearm. Black liquid drips from the puncture, but the motion releases Cattia.

Cattia falls forward and Rachel snarls. Her bloody nails claw at the knife lodged in her arm, digging to remove the burning blade. Cattia drops and scurries along the floor. She gasps for air and crawls to escape the line of fire. Only Rachel aims it at me. If I duck Calix is behind me. I freeze. Cold sweat moistens the back of my shirt. The blade releases as Brett jumps in front. I reach my arms around her waist to push her down against the floor. I squeeze my eyes shut and pray Calix is not in the way and I'm not too late to save Brett. I wait for the heat of the blade to strike me, for Brett to scream, and Calix to fall.

My chest tightens at the thought of living without them. Brett, the spitting image of my mother. I can't lose her to Caradoc's darkness. It's my duty to protect her. When we were separated I had to believe she could take care of herself. Reunited a few days ago, I barely had the chance to have her alone. My mom fought for us. My father left to protect us in the hope that Caradoc would spare our lives. Calix. He trained me for a life I did not come prepared for. I can't do it without him. The warmth of his body against mine is still fresh. Now I'll never know how things could end up. The possibility of a future cut away by a blade.

Light courses through my veins and ignites inside of me. A dull burn at the pain of losing everyone I fought for. Everyone I love. The pressure behind my eyes releases fresh tears.

I want to surrender, but I can't. I have to fight for my family, my blood. I flinch away from Rachel, the thought of her standing so close, the havoc she's determined to cause, the possibility of death and war. I drag Brett's body with me.

I look up, readying myself for the fatal blow, prepared to meet the eyes of my killer, but my mind can't put it together. Rachel's body slumps over. The throwing knife sticks out of her chest, pinning her to the stone wall. Images of possibilities whirls through my head as I imagine what happened. Cattia sobs next to Rachel on the floor, mourning the darkness that extracted their friendship. I'm numb, unable to understand what happened as I focus my worry on Brett.

I flip Brett's body over and check for wounds. My hands work down her stomach and over her legs, rummaging through fabric for the blade or blood. Her lips are split and her cheek bruised.

"Can you quit it!" she whines. A quick glance and I register she's fine, but my thoughts don't stop searching.

I roll over to check Calix. My view lines up with his knees from the floor. My chest relaxes. He hasn't collapsed. He's not injured. An image of an arrow in his temple flashes through my mind. I peer up, scared at what I might find.

He smirks down at me. Humour dances across his features, but his mouth bows in shock. The look he sends me when he can't think of a sarcastic comeback fast enough.

I whirl around to Brett. "Why would you jump in front of me? Are you stupid!" I scold. She snickers. "What is up with you two! We're close to death!"

I glance between their smiles and around the arena. Descendants gawk, their eyes sullen from battle, but their brows raised. Grey skinned bodies cover the arena floor in heaps of fighting gear. Faces of those who fought for the balance of light lost at the darkness of someone else. Drenched weapons line the bleachers in spots of red. The truth hangs in the air and I don't have to ask to know Caradoc fled. His followers abandoned on the ground with their limbs sprawled in different directions.

Then I see it. A thin film glimmers in the light. It shakes as dust flitters against it. The invisible field expands from Brett to Calix. It circles around us in a protective shield. I extend a finger outward, expecting the film to break. It feels solid under my touch. My finger rebounding off the translucent layer. It holds like rounded glass.

"Well, fuck," Onyx says from a few bleachers down.

"It appears there are a few exceptions to affinity and balance," Zilla muses.

Offbeat intakes of breath echo around the gym. My pulse quickens. Affinity? Brett hugs me in excitement. She sends words of encouragement that I don't hear. Calix massages wide arches along my back, cooing how it will all turnout okay and to let the shield fall.

The orb disappears. Like the pop of a bubble it's gone, releasing Calix and Brett.

"How?" I whisper.

"Everyone triggers differently, you will train the Sense to better understand it," Zilla says.

The room bursts into shouts of victory, roars of jittery laughter and whoops of "did you see that?" Voices holler across the bleachers demanding assistance and calling the names of their friends. Preceptors and instructors rush to help Descendants in pain. Everyone offers aid as we work to escort the injured to the weapon room to bathe in the healing tub.

I help Brett to her feet. Calix touches my back as we step down the bleachers. So this is it, the battle is over. Caradoc is gone. His followers are dead. My sister is safe, Calix is okay, my friends are here. I have an affinity.

Calix drops to the ground and screams. I round on my feet, raising my arms to catch him.

Julius appears and lifts Calix up. Calix's body convulses. His shoulders shake, his head lolls, his legs have gone limp. He sprawls on the floor. His eyes roll back and foam surfaces from his lips. His lashes quiver, unable to close.

"Check for injury!"

"Has he been hurt?"

"Calix!"

I don't realize the last voice I hear is my own. Bodies rush around him and shove me out from the huddle. I hear fabric rip as his clothes tear away. I glimpse his bare chest through the shoulders that block him in. Descendants circle around, linking arms to form a cage. Julius' hands work over his bare skin, searching for the source of pain. Others shout that he is one of them. That he rejected balance.

"No!" I shout, but no one hears. Calix risked his life for me and Brett. He's lived here since he was thirteen. He wouldn't give up.

"Traitor."

"Snake."

Crystal's words roll over my mind. Find the deception and get rid of it. The deception in the forest took the form of a snake. Mary-Anne, Caradoc's daughter, refused eye contact and failed Sound—two notions of demon exposure. Then later, when Calix surfaced from the healing pool the wind screamed a warning through the bleachers. It did not affect those who rejected light. Sound, the Sense that alerts the truth and informs us of the deception. Mary-Anne did not know the truth because she could not hear it. She changed when Sound first entered the dome and I raced to save Calix, battered in the woods. She triggered the reveal of Caradoc's followers. She is the deception. Trained by her father to lead his unorthodox cause. Her thin frame is evidence for a loss of appetite. Her cower an act to hide her weakness. Her twitch confirms the fight against the destruction of balance Caradoc raised in her.

"It's not him!" No one listens. I pray to the angels and God, crying up to my mother for help and guidance.

Then it stops. The air turns still. No one breathes.

What did they do?

"No!"

I shove through their arms and reach for him. The circle opens and I stumble through. I fall to the floor. Tears streak my cheeks. Who fired the last shot?

I stop. My threats lost on my lips. A breath stuck in my throat. My hand shakes as I brush his hair from his forehead. His skin is hot. He doesn't move. I shake him. My eyes dart between the faces in the circle. Some Descendants from this camp, others I don't recognize. No one explains or offers help. Their expressions wiped clean from emotion. Their gazes blank. They all wear a mask of content.

I wipe the tears from Calix's cheek, knowing they're my own. His lashes flutter under my touch and I whisper his name with every breath over and over. The sharp arch of his nose almost touches mine as I carry him in my lap. His eyes flutter open. I gasp.

Expecting his usual brown eyes to look into mine and the familiar smirk to lift his lips is stupid of me. He's changed. The air feels cold and the moment freezes. Descendants step back and I move closer, wanting to help. His hot skin wraps around my wrist in the thin lines of his fingers. I don't pull away. I can't.

I sniffle. He tilts his head towards mine, and blows minty breaths. How he managed to smell good after battle and transformation, I cannot fathom. I want to roll my eyes and offer a half-witted comment, but he won't understand. He's not the same. He peers at me, his expression patient, waiting for me to explain why I gawk at him. I wait for the joke that teases me about his good looks and for him to call out my fangirl actions.

"Why the paparazzi?" I don't have to turn around to know he points at the people behind me.

"Calix, you're glowing," I say.

"This is no time for subtleties, Belle. Calling me sexy isn't hard to do," he says.

"No, Calix, you're *glowing*." I dig my nails into his ribs, pulling him closer.

His eyes are no longer brown but a deep molten gold. His black hair hangs in hue of light. A dull halo films his body as if the light reflects against his skin. His bare chest rises, no longer pale white but a yellowish-brown tan. His teeth gleam from under his full lips. The scar on his head shimmers as if formed by specks of metal. The same metallic glint stretches across his bicep as if written in golden ink.

"Aggelos," Julius translates the script.

"It appears the bell has cried. The centre inscribes the heart of the direct Descendant," Zilla recites the prophecy. The circle collapses around us. One by one, Descendants take their knee.

Heads bow forward. Shoulders slant up the bleachers towards us.

Angel.

Chapter 25

"Don't go," I grip Brett's sleeve and force her into another hug. She mutters something against my shoulder. Her squished mouth leaves her words distorted.

"Stop suffocating her!" Onyx cries out from behind me. I shoot her a look.

Brett uses the distraction to free herself and I pull her into me before she can take another step. One quick squeeze then I let her go. I ruffle her hair. "I'll see you soon," I tell her. My chest tightens at my weak attempt at positivity. The next solstice is half a year away. The Preceptors plan to utilize the gap of time until the next Summoning to discuss new protection tactics and planned exercises to strengthen the current balance of the camps. "Take care of yourself," I say. Brett nods.

"Not all of us are a human shield." Brett nudges a small fist against my shoulder.

"I told you if you ever came to Force with a shield I'd beat you with it, so you one up me and become one." Lara rolls her eyes and her R's. Her face is puffy and I know she misses her brain sister. She's slept roughly the past couple of nights. We all have. The injuries closed but the memories of battle are a fresh pain. I link my arm through Lara's in silent reassurance. Brett is alive; I should not take it for granted.

"Before I forget—" Brett reaches into her bag to pull something out "—here." She holds out my yellow sweater. The one she wore the last day I saw her. My lips twitch and my eyes prickle.

"Keep it, kid." I shove it towards her. *Remember me*, I want to tell her. She reaches to zip her bag closed. A smirk lifts her lips in a look that asks, *How can I forget?*

"You're a pain in my ass," I call to Brett as she steps towards the train. *I love you.*

"Love you, too," she returns. She parades onto the ramp, following the flow of Descendants as they heave on bags of luggage. The car doors swoosh open in front of her. Her blonde-streaked hair ruffles over her backpack, Onyx's dye job well done. I smirk at the memory of Brett squirming under tinfoil clippings.

And then the doors close.

Lara lightly presses her hand on my shoulder. My stomach knots and I swallow. I got the chance to say goodbye. I know she is at a regional camp and safe. She will practice and grow into an affinity. I know that now, but it still hurts.

"Can I have a moment to say goodbye?" a rough voice asks. Lara removes her hand.

Jeremy approaches. His walk confident. "Isabelle." His eyes glint with approval as he looks me over. I open my mouth then snap it shut. "Don't," he says, humour leaving his features. "You know I love you." He holds up flat palms. "I know you love me. And I will always remember everything you've done for me. We're on a different path, I know that, too. What I am trying to say is, I will always be here for you, anytime. I'm going to miss you." He wraps his arms around me. I never have to ask him for a hug; he always knows when I need one.

I let go. "It's your time to lead, Jarebear. You are going to do great." I smile, unsure if it reaches my cheeks. He pulls me into another hug.

"You're not a broken bell anymore, you never were. You didn't need us to feel whole, you just thought you did. But the truth is we always needed you. I know you don't believe that, but it's true. I have always known you were special." His lips brush against my hair.

"I'm going to miss you." My eyes water.

"I'm not going anywhere." He squeezes my arm before he lets go.

I watch as the train doors shut behind him. I follow his buzzed hair through the windows of the train as he takes a seat next to Brett. They wave through the window, and Brett makes funny faces. A train horn slices through the air as the engine rumbles. The tires screech and the cars pull away. I cross my arms around my torso as if fastening myself together to avoid breaking.

The train disappears into the tree line behind Ordnance. I cradle my chest to keep my heart from shattering.

Calix stands on the other side of the tracks. His tall, slim frame and broad shoulders slump casually against a tree. The setting sun paints the sky orange. His skin glows a soft gold. Its own ray of sunlight. He ducks his head and kicks the dirt, peeking up at me from a distance. The last few days since he changed he's gone through different meetings with Preceptors. Different discussions and minds working to piece together the cause of his condition. All the while Calix patiently waited for me to digest the situation and offered me the time to spend with Brett. His real fear is the uncertainty of whether I think him developing a golden hue is a turn-off, but not wanting to ask. He lingers, as if expecting an answer of what I might feel, but not wanting to risk asking the question.

I cross over the tracks, removing the remaining space between us and closing the emotional gap in his mind. The wind sings "The Song from the Trees."

Calix smirks as I approach. His gold eyes rest warm on my face. They'll take some getting used to. That I can admit.

His tan skin contrasts the dark bark of the tree. His black hair hangs over his metallic scar. I shoot him the finger and scrunch my nose. He chuckles.

"I guess this means we're stuck with each other," he says, his lips curling.

"I fail to see the problem from your end. However, I will accept your condolences to me." He twirls a strand of my hair. The curl wraps perfectly around his index finger.

"Hey, at least your protector in battle can shoot straight." He doesn't move his eyes away from the coil of my hair.

"Yeah, but my partner glows in the dark. Dead giveaway. I can only take you out in the daylight." I step closer, crossing my arms.

"You'll never lose me now."

"You say that like it's a good thing."

"Hey, that's the direct Descendant you're talking to!"

"Who says I want you—" He presses his lips to mine, cutting off my empty threats and spurts of profane slander. His fingers work to uncross my arms. His solid chest flattens against me, erasing the space between us until there's none left. My pulse quickens and my veins ignite, melting my body into the heat of his.

"Yeah, girl, get some!"

"Woooo!"

Onyx and Lara holler in the distance. Whistles sing through the air. Calix laughs against my lips. I smile, but lack that kind of dedication. I break the kiss and spin around to find my friends with their hands cupped around their mouths for another round of wolf howls. Onyx shoves Julius and he pushes her back. The two engage in a swatting fight. Their hands fling aimlessly at each other in laughter. Ash's fingers link through Brody's. The two stand confident, the battle of death casting a new light on the battle of gay openness. Oliver nuzzles his face against Lara's cheek, his tattooed arms wrap around her waist eliminating the subtleties of a bilingual romantic code.

Calix pinches my chin and steers my face to his. His lips brush against mine, resuming our kiss, but stopping short to look at me. His palm cups my cheek. The halo of his skin blurs our surroundings into a moment of light. He tugs on a curl, winding it around his finger in endless loops. His untamed hair tickles my forehead as he leans down against me. A breath of spearmint never smelt sweeter. The wind wraps around us in a soft song, binding us together in the warm embrace of the breeze. The trees shake in a dance and the sun drips a gold spotlight onto the green grass stage.

So maybe there is sin in all of us, but a summer at Bible camp will teach you to punch a demon. And in Calix's case, how to become an angel.

Tempore.

The End

Made in the USA
Columbia, SC
13 June 2017